"Demorg!"

Chip Demory jumped. When he heard the voice again, louder and more urgent, he dashed back to the bench.

"Where are you going? That's not your name," Tom called, but Chip ignored him.

"Demorg, where have you been?" demanded the coach. Without waiting for an answer, he shoved Chip toward the field. "Ruiz has the wind knocked out of him. Take over at left linebacker!"

"Go get 'em, Chip!"

At Left Linebacker, Chip Demory

NATE AASENG

Chariot Books
David C. Cook Publishing Co.

To the memory of Gladys Bull

A White Horse Book
Published by Chariot Books,
an imprint of David C. Cook Publishing Co.
David C. Cook Publishing Co., Elgin, Illinois 60120
David C. Cook Publishing Co., Weston, Ontario

AT LEFT LINEBACKER, CHIP DEMORY
© 1983 by Nathan Aaseng

Cover illustration by Paul Turnbaugh
Cover design by Loran Berg
First Print, 1983
Printed in the United States of America
92 91 90 89 88   3 4 5 6 7

Library of Congress Cataloging-in-Publication Data

Aaseng, Nathan.
  At left linebacker, Chip Demory.

  Previous ed. cataloged under title: 42 red on four.
  Summary: Chip has to choose between being a newly
popular football player and his old moral values.
  [1. Football—Fiction] I. Title.
PZ7.A13Aac 1988   [Fic]   87-30905
ISBN 1-55513-921-3

Contents

1
Doorway to the Unknown

There was no reason for the shove. The hallway that wound into the locker room was narrow, but two boys should still have been able to walk down it side by side without bumping shoulder pads.

It couldn't have been an accident, Chip Demory thought. Eric Youngquist had deliberately knocked him into the wall tiles.

The two had both arrived late for practice, so they found themselves alone in the dimly lit corridor. Searching Eric's face for some explanation, Chip held back for a moment. Had Eric turned and walked away, Chip would have ignored the whole thing. Instead, there stood Eric, leering and blocking Chip's path to the room. So Chip found himself shoving back, and he heard the clack of shoulder pads as Eric backed into the wall. Without hesitation, Eric took his turn again, with a harder push than before. The football gear cushioned the blows, and Chip recovered quickly and lashed out again at his opponent.

This is stupid; it could go on forever, he thought. What's more, it didn't make any sense. Eric Young-quist was nothing but a name and a face to him. What could he have against him? Chip couldn't remember even talking to him before. Dropping his blue helmet on the concrete floor, he braced himself for another round of attacks. Eric grabbed him by the shoulder.

Then, suddenly, it was as though a plug had been pulled. Eric's last shove faded into a harmless nudge. Without a word, Chip's mysterious attacker turned and disappeared, still smirking, into the locker room.

As Chip watched him go, he felt the warmth of the blood that had rushed to his cheeks and the tips of his ears. *That probably wasn't a smart thing to do,* he thought. Eric was bigger than he, and, Chip assumed, probably a lot stronger. But what else could you do when someone came at you like that?

Chip had seen the white block letters that spelled "locker room" above the door for as long as he had been attending Forest Grove School, but he had never been in the room before. He couldn't remember when he had made the final decision to step through the doors and join the football team. All he knew was that he was tired of being a nobody. The athletes seemed to be the ones who had it made, and Chip had finally decided he was going to join them. The way he had it figured, that uniform held the key to something. Respect, perhaps. Maybe even popularity.

When he thought of the evening he had broken the news to his dad, he felt he was already halfway toward his goals. The announcement had caught his dad by surprise at the supper table; the man had held that mouthful of food a long time before swallowing. Chip's

8

dad had never tried to push him into sports, but he couldn't hide the fact that he was pleased.

"Sounds like fun," his dad had said. "What made you decide to try it?"

Chip had shrugged. "Like you said, it sounded like fun." There had been no reason to go into all of his motives.

"Is there a group of you boys in on this?" Dad had asked. No, he had done this on his own. Most of his current friends weren't the football type. Sometimes he was almost ashamed to know them. Take Tom, for instance. He was a nice enough guy, went to church, was good at music. But sometimes he was so innocent it was embarrassing.

"Can you imagine Tom in football pads?" he had said with a laugh. "Jason might be coordinated enough to play, but not Tom . . ."

"Well, I know *you'll* enjoy it, anyway," his dad had smiled. "I sure did!"

As he prepared to turn the last of three corners in the entranceway, Chip hoped that his dad was right.

The room turned out to be nothing but a long galley, packed with boys. Since the benches ran parallel with the lockers instead of facing the blackboard, everyone sat crowded on the floor on either side of the benches as Coach Ray Marsh stood before the blackboard. There were no showers, but that did not matter to the Forest Grove football team. Everyone was expected to change into football gear at home. In fact, the only way they used the room was as a meeting place.

The strange newness of the situation seemed frightening. Chip shifted his weight from one foot to the other, as if pulled by two magnets, as he tried to decide whether or not to stay. Finally he walked forward and knelt on the floor at the back of the group.

The coach had a wide face and short neck, which made him appear large when he was actually of average size. He certainly dressed the part of a coach, from his navy blue Windbreaker and white shorts to his high, white socks and heavy, black shoes. Chip wondered about the shoes. Why would a guy need special football shoes with cleats just to coach?

Had Chip been less self-conscious, he would have stood instead of knelt. He wasn't one of the larger boys, and he had trouble seeing over the group from his spot in the back. Coach Ray had been talking for some time now, but Chip hadn't heard much of what he said. He kept debating whether or not to sneak out and forget this crazy notion. But while he scanned the rows of white-jerseyed boys to see if anyone would notice his exit, he was suddenly jolted by a familiar face. Eric, in the back of the pack on the other side of the bench, was watching him with that same smirk.

Chip quickly turned away and started to concentrate on what the coach was saying. "Listen up now, boys. This is a big group and there's no way I can try and coach you all by myself. So I want you to meet Bronc Galloway. He'll be helping me out this year."

Bronc Galloway must have been stretched out on the floor in the front of the group, for Chip had not noticed him before. As the man stood up, Chip wondered how he could have missed him. It took no imagination to see this man in football gear in a starting lineup in high school or college. Under his sweater a huge chest puffed out, so large that his arms did not hang comfortably at his sides. Although Bronc appeared to be no older than his mid-thirties, he was almost bald, with only a few surviving hairs clinging to his temples. He wore gray, cuffed pants that had large loops for a belt, but no belt was there. The man snapped his gum so vigorously that he reminded Chip of a dog crunching his dinner.

"How're ya doin'!" grinned Bronc between chomps.

"OK, fellas," said Coach Ray, stepping in front of

10

Bronc. "I want all the backs to come with me, and the linemen to go with Bronc. Let's go and have ourselves a good practice!"

As Chip followed the stream of boys out of the locker room, he felt a wave of panic. *I thought the coaches told you where to play,* he thought. Everyone else seemed to know exactly where they were going as the team split into two sections and jogged out on the grass, but Chip stood still, trying to decide which of the departing groups to join. He had never thought of himself as a back; only the really good players got to carry the ball. But then he might be overpowered by the larger boys who played in the line. A last look at Bronc sent him scurrying to Coach Ray's side of the field. As long as he had a choice, Chip would shy away from that tough-looking brute.

Taking his usual spot at the end of a line, Chip wished for the hundredth time that one of his friends had come out for football. When he saw the players in line ahead of him fastening their helmets, he felt more foolish than ever. He hadn't been wrong about the better players taking to the backfield. There was Rennie Ruiz, the fastest runner in school. Bruce Wilkes was always the first person chosen for any sport in phys. ed. class. And nobody ever thought about trying to win the quarterback job away from Scot Schultz, who had a throwing arm like a missile launcher.

Coach Ray blew his whistle for silence even though no one was saying a word. He pulled out two rolls of tape from his pocket and tossed them to the boys. "Print your names, big enough so I can read 'em."

Most of the others paired off and used a friend's back to write on. But Chip bent down with one knee on the grass. His thigh pad was hard enough to make a good support, and he started to print on the piece he had torn off the roll.

While Scot's back was being used, he glanced in

11

Chip's direction. "Not your first name," he advised. "Coach likes last names."

Chip nodded, tore off another piece of tape and shakily printed "Demory." The exchange had reminded him that most of these players had been out for football before. There was more to joining a football team than just walking through the locker room door. *What am I doing here?* he wondered again.

After the group had run through tires and caught passes, Coach Ray grabbed a blocking dummy. "Some of you come and hold these," he said as he dragged one to the middle of the field. With swift cooperation, four dummies were soon lined up, five yards apart. Chip saw Bruce clutch the football and plow into the first dummy. There was a loud grunt as the boy hit the object and charged quickly toward the next.

"Well, here goes," gulped Chip, fumbling the football that Coach Ray had tossed to him. He picked it up and ran toward the first dummy, which was held by the coach. The collision stunned him. Those fluffy-looking bags were a lot more solid than they looked! Chip's helmet slipped over his nose. He took a step back and adjusted it before continuing to the other targets, which were held by other players.

"No, no, no!" shouted Coach Ray, rushing in front of the startled boy. The coach grabbed Chip's helmet and turned it slightly to see the name taped to it. "Demorg," he said in a softer voice, as if the patience he was showing took massive self-control.

"It's Demory, not Demorg," mumbled Chip.

The coach stared hard at the helmet and shrugged. "That's the darndest *y* I ever saw; looks like a *g* to me. OK, Demory, you were doing it all wrong. I didn't see any drive. For cryin' out loud, I don't want you to lie down on the bag, I want you to hit it. Here, watch me!" he said, shoving the bag at Chip.

From a standing start, he blew his whistle and

charged forward. The collision nearly blasted Chip off his feet. "Hit hard!" the coach puffed. "Legs pumping, always pumping. Spin away, charge, hit again. Now you try it. Hit! Legs going, legs going! Pump those legs, Demorg! Hit! Spin away! Charge! Legs!" Chip's turn probably lasted no longer than fifteen seconds, but he was relieved to take his turn holding up a dummy. Each player took two more runs through the drill. Chip felt his second and third tries must have been a little better; at least he wasn't yelled at as much.

No sooner had he popped into the last dummy than the whistle blew, summoning them for yet another drill. The group spread out into three widely spaced lines facing Coach Ray. At his command, they all ran in place, awaiting further commands. In rapid succession, the coach pointed left, then right, then to the ground, then left. The boys tried to keep up with his motions, running in the direction he was pointing, dropping to the ground when he pointed down. Within a few minutes, everyone had fallen hopelessly behind. It was obvious that no one cared for this drill.

"Coach, why are we doing this?" groaned Scot as he slumped to his knees. "What does it have to do with football?"

"We're doing it because I think it's a good idea," smiled the coach. "And because it's good for you. Let's go again! Left! Right!" A few minutes later he grinned and said, "Everyone around the goalpost, on the double, then report to where the linemen are."

Had Chip worn a watch to practice, his eyes would have been on it every thirty seconds. When he had been thinking about playing football this fall, he had expected some hard work. But this tedious, nerve-wracking routine was hardly worth it. Whatever excitement he had felt when he first put on the helmet and uniform had long since worn off. Although the slow trot around the posts seemed a waste of time, Chip enjoyed every second away from the coach and his drills.

When they returned to Coach Ray, he surveyed them with a sly smile. "One last drill for you, and then you can go home. Bronc, set up the bags for the one-on-one drill." The assistant swung around two bags, one in each hand, and set them on a worn stretch of grass, about six feet apart.

"I want the linemen over by the dummies, backs over here," said Coach Ray. "This is a simple exercise. You backs are to try to run between the bags. You linemen are to try to stop them. If the back gets through, he's done with practice, and the lineman goes to the end of his line. If the lineman makes the tackle, he's through for the day and the back gets in line. Any questions?"

There were none. It was all painfully clear to Chip. But for the first time, Chip found some competition for the last spot in the line. Two boys had quietly sneaked around and were now behind him. Chip glanced at the long string of linemen waiting to get their chance. He could be stuck running at them all afternoon while all the other backs went home.

Rennie looked as concerned about the drill as a cat settling down for a nap. Hands on his hips, he waited for Coach Ray to give him the ball. At the sound of the ever-present whistle, he flipped the ball from his left hand to his right, and started forward at an easy pace. A lineman crouched three yards in front of the dummies, his arms held out from his chest like a wrestler. Rennie put on a burst of speed to his right. When the lineman tried to cut him off, Rennie swerved sharply to the other side. Lurching off balance, the lineman tried to dive back, and made a desperate swipe at the speedster with his arm. But Rennie easily hopped over it and trotted between the dummies.

"Nice running," said the coach, clapping. "That

14

was a pretty piece of work, Ruiz. See you tomorrow. Next!"

I'm going to be the only one who doesn't make it, thought Chip. He saw Bronc whisper something to the boy who had missed the tackle. Then the assistant coach patted him on the pads and sent him to the end of the line. "That's going to be me," Chip muttered.

Another whistle blast brought Chip's attention back to the drill. Perry Clyde Brown, who liked to be called P.C., didn't exactly leap forward at the signal. Roosevelt Baxter was blocking his path, and he seemed to take up most of the room between the dummies. By far the largest kid in their grade, he had proven on many occasions that very little of his great bulk was fat.

P.C. rocked forward several times, then finally lowered his head and took off. Despite his determination, the huge arms of Roosevelt Baxter wrapped around him and slammed him to the ground. As P.C. hobbled to his feet, Coach Ray nodded his approval. "Good, clean tackle. That's the way to do it."

P.C. refused to let the hard hit silence him. Returning to the sympathetic group of backs, he muttered, "Welcome, to the 'Get Canned by Baxter Club.' It's always the same. Every time we do this drill, I get stuck with good old Roosevelt. Why doesn't anyone else get Roosevelt?" He tapped the helmet of the boy in front of him in line. "Isn't this fun? Boy, I can't think of anything I enjoy more on a nice day like this than being annihilated by somebody five times my size!"

For the first time that day, Chip joined in with the laughter as P.C. sputtered on about his misfortune. The smile had vanished, however, by the time he had worked his way to the front of the line. P.C. Brown wasn't the only one victimized by fate. Chip saw that the lineman he would have to beat was Eric! He still wore that same goofy sneer, although it was harder to detect underneath his helmet. With a deep breath,

Chip took off for the blocking dummies.

"Hey, wait a minute!" shouted Coach Ray. "You forgot the football. And I'd appreciate it if you'd wait for the whistle next time." Chip was too paralyzed with fear and embarrassment to come up with a plan for getting around Eric. After starting forward, he stopped and began to lean to the left to fake out the defender. But he had barely moved his head when Eric rushed forward and grabbed him just above the knees. Neatly picking him off the ground, he carried him toward the row of backs until the coach whistled for him to stop. Chip ducked back in line, too humiliated to even look up from the grass. "Next!" screamed the coach.

I might just as well put wimp *on my helmet instead of my name,* Chip thought bitterly. It had been a crushing lesson, but Chip had learned from that run. The next time he got the ball, he didn't waste time with timid fakes. He drove straight for the defender, and the two fell over each other. He didn't get through that time, either, but at least he hadn't been picked off the ground like a kindergartner.

P.C. finally got a break on his fourth try. He had been paired with the smallest lineman, and he could hardly wait to try his luck. As he burst through the defender and dove between the tackling dummies, he let out a whoop. "What power! What a runner! Sorry all you pro scouts, but I'm not signing anything until my agents look over your offers."

There were only two running backs left in line when Chip finally succeeded. He tore through an attempted tackle and sprinted past the dummies, feeling as though a huge load had slid off his shoulders. But he noted, bitterly, that none of the good players were around to see him break through. Besides, being the next-to-last to succeed was hardly an achievement.

Chip slammed his helmet on the sparse turf and

kicked it toward the school. Football was supposed to be his chance to prove he wasn't a dork. Instead it had proved, beyond a doubt, that he really was.

2
A Private War

Chip watched the last orange bus rumble off from in front of the school. Holding his breath until the exhaust fumes had drifted away, he sat on the steps in front of the glass doors of the entrance. He held a wadded Windbreaker in his hand; the day had turned out warmer than he had expected when he had left the house that morning.

Those guys are going to bake in practice today, he thought, *especially in those dark helmets.*

Chip had not quit the team. True, there were still about half a dozen times each practice when he wished he had never pushed open that locker room door. But it had been his decision to play football, and he felt it his duty to stick it out to the end. After all, he had told everyone that he was a football player. The best thing to do was just to get through the season, suffering in silence. At least none of his family or friends knew how

18

badly he was botching things.

Then, too, there was still hope that things would change. He had overheard Bruce say that after the first few weeks, football started to get fun.

Despite this, it was a relief to be getting out of practice. Coach Ray had happened to schedule a practice for an afternoon when Chip was supposed to meet with the dentist. It was strange to feel almost glad to have a dentist appointment as an excuse.

A car engine rumbled noisily, and Chip stood up to see if it was his ride coming. No, it was a pickup truck, hardly what his sister would be driving. As he absently watched the dust kicked up by the truck, he thought of the practice field again. The lack of rain had hardened the ground so that his football gear didn't seem to be enough protection from hard falls. He was thinking back on one hard tackle when he heard a shout. "Hey, Chip!"

Leaning out the window of the truck, snapping his gum as always, Bronc waved at him. "You look like you need a ride somewhere. Want a lift? Practice won't start for another fifteen minutes."

"No, thanks," Chip said. "My sister should be here any minute. We have to go to the dentist."

"Going to get your fangs sharpened, huh? I knew you were a tiger on the field, but isn't that carrying it a bit too far?" Chip grinned at the attempted joke and shook his head. "Well, see you tomorrow," Bronc said. He waved and turned into the parking lot. Suddenly his truck lurched to a stop. The bald head poked out the window again. "Hey, Chip! What's the deal with you and Eric?"

Chip felt a shiver at the mention of that hated name. Before he could even think about it, he found himself denying it. "There's no problem," he shrugged. He had never imagined that anyone else knew about that trouble.

19

"Come on," frowned Bronc. "Hey, I've seen you two go at it whenever you get a chance. I mean, the fur is really flyin' in those one-on-one drills. There's got to be something causing that."

"You'd have to ask him," Chip said coldly. "I don't even know him that well, but that's the way he wants it, so—"

Bronc shook a finger at him. "I think we're goin' to have to get you two to talk it out sometime. It's not good when—What in the blue blazes is this?"

The squealing of tires as a Chevy swerved into the parking lot, barely clinging to the road, made Chip wince. "It's my sister," he said, bouncing down the steps.

Bronc had stopped chewing and stared, open-mouthed at the car. "Your sister! Sounds like one tough lady behind the wheel."

"That's the second time she's done that," said Chip. "At least this time it wasn't in front of a parking lot full of people heading into church."

"Oh, yeah?" Bronc smiled. "What church?"

"Trinity," answered Chip, feeling a little uncomfortable. Football and church were two areas of his life Chip had not wanted to mix. He was trying to think of a safe topic of conversation when Bronc changed the subject for him. "So, does she always drive like that?" the coach asked.

"I hope not," answered Chip with a grin. "See you later." He jogged around to the passenger side of the car and climbed in. "What are you trying to do anyway, Jill?" he asked the girl. "You're driving like the Indy 500!"

Jill swept back her long hair and looked at her watch. Chip knew she was embarrassed because of the way she refused to meet his eyes. "I'm in a hurry," she said. "We have only five minutes to get to the dentist's office, and it's a ten-minute drive." After a few seconds of silence, she finally peeked over at him and sighed. "Guess I did take the corner too fast. Well, live and learn. How long have I had a license—five months? Can't expect to be perfect yet. You know what, though," she added, almost in a whisper. "If Dad saw me do that, he wouldn't let me have the car again for about three eternities."

"I don't know why he lets you loose on the road at all," laughed Chip.

"Don't give me a hard time! Mom's got the flu, and Dad doesn't get home until 5:30. Besides, I need the practice."

"You sure picked a great time to practice. Right at the start of rush hour!"

Jill gave him a quick punch in the shoulder. "Quiet. You're making me nervous!"

"Who was the bald guy?" asked Jill, after announcing their arrival to the receptionist. "The one in the pickup. What an ape!"

Chip looked around at the sparse office furnishings. Except for a small coatrack, a window that looked out onto a row of car fenders, a table heaped with magazines, and half a dozen chairs, the room was empty. Pulling up one of the chairs, he said, "You mean the man in the truck that you almost hit?"

"I did not! It wasn't even close. Was he your football coach?"

"He still is, for all I know," said Chip. "At least, he's one of them. He's not a bad guy. I'm beginning to like him better than the other one we've got."

"I've had all kinds of coaches," shrugged Jill. "Somehow I've survived. So, how are you liking football?"

Chip felt important when his sister talked to him. Although they had their differences, and she talked too much for his liking, he'd seen other big sisters in action, and had to admit that he was lucky. At least Jill wasn't afraid to admit, once in a while, that he existed.

"Football's great!" he replied. He felt funny saying it, but he couldn't tell her what he really thought.

"You know, that's one sport I've never been able to figure out. I've gone to a few high school games, but if it weren't for the cheering, I wouldn't even know who's winning."

"That's because it's such a complicated game," explained Chip. "You see, you've got all kinds of games going on at once. Both sides are making secret plans, and there's passing, running, blocking, and tackling all going on at the same time." Chip was starting to feel more fired up about the game than he had in a long time.

"I figured there must be something to it, the way Dad loves to watch it," said Jill. "It sounds like fun. I'll bet you're glad you finally tried out for it this year."

Feeling uncomfortable with the false impression he was giving, Chip changed the subject. "So, do you like volleyball?"

"Love it," Jill grinned. "I think I like it even better than tennis, and you know how I've always loved tennis."

"It's easy to like something when you're great at it," sniffed Chip.

Jill turned on him, irritated. "That isn't true. I'd still like playing those sports even if I wasn't . . ." Seeing that she had been led into a conceited statement, she blushed. "Besides, I'm not all that great."

"Oh, sure!" scoffed Chip. "You're all-conference in tennis, and probably will be in volleyball, too."

"I do all right. You'll probably star at football."

"Don't make me laugh," grumbled Chip.

Jill squinted at the ceiling for a few seconds, as if mulling over something. "Wait a minute. If you really think you're no good at football, why do you say it's such a great game?"

Chip shifted uneasily in his chair. Jill was getting a lot closer to the truth than he could stand. "Oh, who says football is so great?"

"Well, it wasn't me! You're the one who went on and on about it. I don't know which is worse, getting my teeth drilled or trying to make sense out of you. Give me one of those magazines."

Chip scanned the pile and picked out the two with the least torn covers. "Do you want last year's *Reader's Digest* or the February *Boys' Life*?"

Just then the door creaked open. "Chip Demory?" called the receptionist.

Jill caught the magazines as Chip dumped them in her lap. "I think I've got it figured out," she said as he shuffled toward the door. "You went out for sports because you know how much Dad likes to come and watch me play."

Chip decided there was no need to tell her there was some truth in all her guesses. How could he help but want to trade places with her? Everyone in town knew who Jill Demory was. You could hardly flip through the sports section of the local paper during tennis season without seeing her picture. "Right," he grinned. "I figured if *you* could be a star, anyone could."

"Beat it! I hope the dentist broke his drill and has to use a jackhammer on you!"

"That's enough conditioning, boys. We'd better get going on learning the plays."

Coach Ray's words were like thick steaks thrown to a pack of starved dogs. Chip even joined the rest of the team in their whoops and howls. P.C. scurried through the ranks of players, shaking hands like a politician. "I want to personally congratulate each of the courageous

23

survivors of this—"

"Knock off the clowning!" ordered Coach Ray. "We're going to organize you into units. Now, there's no such thing as a definite first team or second team at this point. Remember, the unit I put you on isn't necessarily the unit you'll stay on all year. It's just that we have to start somewhere. Now, when I call your name, I want you over here. Foster! Baxter! Torberg!"

Chip didn't know much about the linemen, other than Roosevelt and Eric, but he had seen the backs in action for some time. His suspicions of how the team was being divided were confirmed when the names of Ruiz, Wilkes, and Schultz were read off in order. The three pranced over to the coach, trying some awkward high-five handshakes. Then they started slapping hands with the linemen who had been selected.

"Knock it off!" shouted the coach. "I told you, it doesn't mean that you've made the starting team. In fact, the whole lot of you may wind up second-string by our first game!"

P.C. giggled and whispered what everyone else was thinking. "The coach is right. If Wilkes and Schultz break both their legs, they *may* get beaten out for a starting spot."

Coach Ray motioned with his clipboard to where Bronc was pacing in rhythm with his chewing. "I want the following to report to Bronc when I call your name." He stared at his clipboard for a second, as if trying to break the code of whatever was written on it. Finally he plunged into the list of names at a rapid pace. Eight of the eleven were mispronounced so badly that several boys were not sure whether they had been called or not. Chip, however, had heard the name "Demorg" so often that he automatically responded to the title. Trotting to where Bronc was lining up play-ers, he glanced back at the boys who had not been chosen. He felt sorry for that glum group, whose hopes

24

for playing time this year had just been crushed. At the same time, he felt glad, and a little proud, that he had been selected for the second group. At least it showed he wasn't a total loser.

Grabbing Chip by the shoulders, Bronc gave the boy a quick inspection. "You look like a linebacker to me, Chip," he said. "At least you will if you start eatin' three meals a day!" He rapped him lightly on the ribs with his knuckles. "Why don't you take the left linebacker spot?"

Chip was listening to Coach Ray explain to the unchosen players that their role would be to back up the offensive "starters" when he felt a tap on his shoulder. P.C. grabbed him by the pads and marched him to the defensive end on the left side. "Hey! Dave Atkinson! I can't tell if it's you or your twin!"

The tall lineman grinned down at the two of them. "This isn't me; it's him. I'm over there on the right side." He pointed to the gangly figure standing on the other end of the defensive line. "I'll bet it's hard to tell Dave and me apart when we've got our helmets on."

"Actually, Dan, the helmets make it easier," chuckled P.C. Nodding for Chip to come closer, he said, "As we all know, I'm a man of few words, so I'll make it short. We all know each other, at least, sort of. The way I see it, the best way to survive practice is to hang together. If I know this coach, we're stuck on defense for the rest of the year. What's more, we probably won't play much."

He must have caught the question in Chip's expression because he explained, "He likes to have the best players in for both offense and defense, and the best eleven are in that huddle over there. Practice can be a drag when you know you won't get into the games, so here's my idea. Dan, you're the left end, Chip's the left linebacker, and I'm the left cornerback. Let's set up our own game against the right side of the defense. We

25

guard our turf better than they guard theirs, see? Only plays run outside the tackles count; if they run up the middle, we don't count it."

Chip hadn't followed all the details of the plan. He was still thinking about P.C.'s statement that they all knew each other. By name, maybe, but not beyond that. *But then,* he thought, *P.C. seems to think he's good friends with everyone.*

Dan shook his head wearily. Chip had always thought Dan would be a good person to know. He was a brain in class without being either obnoxious or self-conscious about it. Along with his twin Dave, Dan had a better build for basketball than football. But the lanky pair had never found a sport they didn't like. "Your game sounds like fun, I guess," he said in a doubtful voice. "But there's no way for this group to beat the right side."

For a second, Chip thought Dan must be thinking of him as a handicap in this contest. Instinctively he backed away. But then Dan pointed to the huge figure dwarfing his teammates in the offensive huddle. Roosevelt Baxter looked like a playground supervisor hovering over a circle of first graders.

P.C. unsnapped his chin guard and rubbed his chin. "I see the problem. We've got our good buddy Roosevelt blocking against you." Putting an arm around Dan, he said, "On behalf of all of us, I'd like to thank you for sacrificing your life for the good of the team. All right, so you have to play against him. We'll give ourselves a handicap of one yard per play." Before he slipped his mouthpiece back in place, he thumped Chip on the helmet. "Funny, I always thought your name was Demory."

"So did I, but I can't convince the coach," said Chip. "I got tired of arguing about it, so I just don't say anything anymore."

"Don't take it personally," laughed P.C. "He just

26

doesn't get along well with names. Well, I'd better shut up; here they come!"

As P.C. skipped back to his cornerback spot, Chip looked over the rest of the defense. It felt good to finally have a position to play—especially since he wasn't stuck at running back, where he felt out of place. But the best part was being in on P.C.'s little gang. If you couldn't get along with P.C., you couldn't get along with anyone, and Dan seemed nice enough. The problem was, would they put up with him if he made too many mistakes?

Even that worry, however, seemed minor when Chip discovered who was storming around a few feet to his right. Eric had been put at middle linebacker, and it was obvious he wasn't flattered to be there. Despite what the coach said, everyone knew this was the second-string group. Eric thought he belonged on the first team. Much as Chip hated to admit it, he agreed with Eric.

Muttering and spitting, Eric wandered in a wide circle around the defense. Chip tried to back out of his way, but Eric got close enough to recognize him. One look at the menacing glare and Chip turned away, pretending his shoes needed tying. If only he hadn't been placed right next to Eric! What was the kid's problem, anyway? Why was he always looking for a fight?

The offense ran through plays in a drill that seemed as silly as it was boring to Chip. Everyone simply walked through the play. The whole thing reminded Chip of a slow-motion square dance. At least there wasn't much for the defense to do, so Chip could concentrate on staying out of Eric's way. The middle linebacker was still steaming. Rather than let a blocker nudge him to one side, he would just turn his back and looked bored.

After what seemed like several afternoons strung

27

together, Coach Ray finally said, "Let's run through a couple of plays with some real blocking and tackling!"

The glare of the setting sun was getting under Chip's helmet as he watched the offense crowd around the coach in the huddle. Not until they broke their huddle and jogged toward the football to challenge him did he realize how little he actually knew about his position. He had watched football with his dad for years, and had thought he knew the game inside and out. But as the linemen bent toward the ground to get in position, he found that he had no idea what he should do. Eric stood close enough to touch the linemen, while the other linebacker stood several yards behind them. Where was he supposed to play?

Dan turned and called quietly over his shoulder. Unable to hear him, Chip darted up to the tall lineman. "They're coming to this side. Be ready for it," came the warning.

"How do you know?" asked Chip.

"No time now," answered Dan, digging his cleats into what little grass was left on the hardened ground.

Quarterback Scot called out a few numbers and then, in Chip's eyes, the entire field turned into a madhouse. He could make out that the general flow was in his direction. But all the movement distracted him so much that he barely moved from his original spot. There seemed to be nothing to do but wait until the ball carrier arrived and then try and tackle him.

As Chip inched forward, he was spotted by Rennie, who was leading the way for Bruce on the run. With a loud grunt, Rennie threw his body at Chip. Chip managed to keep his feet as Rennie stumbled. But as he was trying to find where Bruce had gone, he was suddenly jolted from behind. He fell forward over Rennie, who kicked at him to get him off. Neither saw P.C. end the play by bumping the ball carrier out-of-bounds after an eight-yard gain.

28

Chip finally untangled himself from Rennie, then cringed when he saw Eric standing over him, pointing a finger in his face. "If you're too wimpy to make a tackle," he sneered, "why don't you get out of the way so someone else can do it!"

Their private war had gone on in total silence up to this point. Whether it was Eric's mocking voice or just the fact that Chip had finally reached his limit, this time Chip was furious. His back hurt from where Eric had run into him, blood was trickling down his calf, and he was embarrassed in front of his new friends. It especially hurt because what Eric had said was true. Chip knew that he had been standing around like a clod. For all practical purposes, the defense did not have a left linebacker.

He spun away from Eric disdainfully. *I'm not afraid of that creep,* he said to himself. *Big shot thinks he's Mr. Tough. I'll show him!*

"That's a lousy way to start, guys," called P.C.

Chip found Dan still sprawled on the ground near the line of scrimmage, and helped him to his feet. "How did you know they would come this way?"

Dan scraped a clump of dirt off of his elbow. "Just a guess, but I'm right more often than not. See, the coach is right-handed, so I thought it would be natural for him to start off the year with a play to his right. Besides, how could he resist running a play behind Roosevelt?" He smiled weakly. "Of course, it doesn't help to know what's coming if you can't stop it."

"So what are they going to do this time?"

"I can't always tell. If I think I have it figured out, I'll let you know. Hey, P.C.," he called to the cornerback. "Why don't you come closer, and help out on those runs?"

"Come on, I can help some, but I have to watch the pass receivers."

"P.C., we watched that offense walk through three

29

million plays in the last hour, and none of them were passes. They haven't learned any pass plays yet!"

"Why didn't I think of that?" said P.C., joining Chip.

"My dad always says to pay attention to the little things," said Dan. "There's more to football than just banging heads."

When Eric shot one of his glares at Chip, this time Chip glared right back. He didn't shy away from the middle; in fact, he moved a few steps closer to Eric. The play was a basic, straight-ahead run. The blocking was so sloppy that no one even touched the middle linebacker. Eric met Bruce head-on, and stopped the fullback's forward progress. But Bruce kept his balance and squirmed ahead for a couple more yards. As defensive help raced in from all sides, Chip saw his chance to get even. Eric's back provided an inviting target, and Chip closed in. Quickly building up speed, he plowed into the growing pile of players, hitting Eric right around the shoulders. Eric lost his grip, and Bruce burst out of the mob for three more yards before being tackled.

"You moron!" shouted Eric, clenching his fists. "You don't even know whose team you're on! What are you doing out for football, anyway?"

Chip braced himself for a possible attack, but Eric made no move.

"Go on, smack him," said Scot, nudging Eric. That was all the encouragement Eric needed.

3
Forty-Two Red On Four

Chip met Eric's wild-eyed charge as best he could, stepping backwards and fending him off with his arm. When Eric finally got a grip on him and swung him around, Chip grabbed Eric's jersey, and the two toppled over. Eric must have been growing frustrated as they rolled around; he kept clenching his fist but couldn't find an unpadded place to swing at. Finally he aimed a punch at Chip's stomach, but Chip squirmed just enough so that he caught the blow on his hip pad.

Chip struggled to get out from under Eric. Surprised that he was finally able to wriggle free, he instinctively tried to wrestle Eric to the ground. But before he could try, he felt a steel grip under his armpits. Bronc swung him away from his enemy while Dan and Roosevelt grabbed Eric. Chip could hear Eric still cursing, and the calm voice of Dan saying, "Leave him alone!"

"Hey, save it for the other team!" barked Coach Ray, stepping into the middle of the scene. "There's no place for that kind of stuff on any football team of mine. I don't want any fights, or any cheap shots. If you guys want to stay on the team, you're going to have to learn to control your tempers!" Then, waving the rest of the group off, he said, "All of you, that's enough for today. Go on home! See you Monday."

Eric seemed to have settled down some, but Chip was growing angrier by the second. Who did Eric think he was, anyway? And what was the coach doing, chewing *him* out? Any idiot could tell it was all Eric's fault. *I don't care if I do get kicked off,* he thought. *In fact, there's nothing I'd like better!*

He felt a shadow as Dan walked by him. The tall left end was keeping an eye on both linebackers, and he seemed to be purposely adjusting his pace to keep between the two. "If you linebackers would quit pounding each other, we wouldn't be looking like such a bunch of idiots on defense," he offered.

"You're not the one who keeps looking like an idiot," said Eric.

Edging Chip away from Eric, Dan said quietly, "This fight probably isn't any of my business. But I think you two are a lot more alike than you realize."

"Thanks for the insult," spat Chip.

"No, I know Eric, and he's not always such a jerk. Not the friendliest guy in the world, but he's not terrible. Did you know that this is *his* first year out for football, too?"

"I hope it's his last."

"Tell me if I'm wrong," said Dan, tugging off his helmet and wiping back his sweaty hair. "Neither of you seemed to have gotten too comfortable with the practice routine yet."

32

"So we're both new," shrugged Chip. "Where's he get off trying to push me around?"

Dan started biting his lips and screwing up his face, making Chip think that he was debating whether to go on with this conversation. Finally he said, "Eric's fighting to get in with the guys. You have to admit it's not easy for him. He's probably as good as any lineman on the first team. Except for Roosevelt." He grinned, displaying a bruise on his forearm. "But Eric can't get the coaches to notice him, because they're busy watching the starters. So what does he do to get in with that group? He picks on someone to show how tough he is."

"We'll see how tough he is!"

"Maybe. But you can tell he wants to get in with the group. He never would have jumped you there if Scot hadn't opened his big mouth."

Trying to follow Dan's logic had taken some of the edge off Chip's anger. "All right, know-it-all, tell me why he doesn't pick on the scrubs who didn't even make the second team."

Dan stopped walking and gave him a sideways look. "Not a know-it-all, just a good guesser, remember? Now, listen: everyone knows the scrubs aren't good players. They may not like it, but they know what their role is. *You* don't know what *your* role is, and that gives Eric a good chance to try to teach you where you belong. Or where he thinks you belong. But don't worry," he said, leaning on the bike rack to change out of his football shoes. "The coaches are bound to find out how good he is, and then he won't have a chip on his shoulder. Your troubles are practically over."

Mine may be over, thought Chip, watching Eric disappear into the school. *But his aren't!*

As the rest of the class filed out into a noisy, jammed hallway, Chip stood by his desk in the back corner of the classroom. While waiting for Tom to collect his

33

books and papers so they could go to band class, he examined his friend. He had done that often lately, trying to see him the way others must see him. As usual, the exercise made him frown. Those clumsy movements, hand-me-down clothes from what must have been a dozen years back, and the obviously home-made haircut marked him as someone who was really out of it. When Chip walked through the halls with Tom, he was beginning to feel awkward. He could just picture people saying, "Is that the best he can do for friends?"

This time, though, Chip couldn't help but notice something else. Tom's forehead was dotted with sweat, and his face seemed a pasty white. "Are you OK?" Chip asked.

"No, I feel sick," said Tom as he slowly gathered his books in his arms.

"Oh, no. Not you, too!" Chip said. The flu bug raging through the city didn't seem to miss anyone. At least half of Forest Grove school had been hit during the past week, he guessed. Chip had been one of the first to fall victim. Fortunately, the illness left him in as big a hurry as it had come. Chip had only been out of school one day, although he stayed out of football practice for two. But while the bug had lasted, it had been miserable.

"Did you feel weak, and have chills, and feel like you were going to throw up?" groaned Tom.

"Exactly. We'd better get you to the nurse fast. If you're like me, you're not just going to feel like throw-ing up, you're going to do it. Here, I'll carry your books for you."

It couldn't have been a pleasant trip for Tom, but Chip rushed him through the hall and up the steps to the nurse's office without an accident. Then he dropped off Tom's books on the nurse's desk and went off to the band room.

Poor guy, thought Chip. *At least he didn't throw up in the hall. Boy, neither of us would have lived that down.*

Later that afternoon, when Chip joined the football practice, he found even more evidence of the illness. The practice field seemed strange, almost ghostly, and not only because someone had marked the sidelines and the ten-yard intervals with chalk. It was as quiet as a funeral home.

Coach Ray marched onto the newly lined turf, staring at his watch. He looked over the sparse groups of white-uniformed boys and frowned. After a blast of his whistle that seemed to echo off the brick walls of the school, he said, "I know there's been a lot of sickness going around, and we're missing quite a few of our numbers. But we have our first game coming up next week, and we can't afford to go on vacation while we wait for everyone to get well. You boys badly need a full-scale scrimmage to give you a feel of this game before I can send you out to play for real."

He threw open a cardboard box and spilled out the blue bib tops. "I want the defense in blue today, so come on and grab a top. I want the offense and defense to go at it just as if this were a real game. Offense, you get four downs to make ten yards. Defense, you get three points every time you force the offense to punt."

As Chip bent down to pick out one of the blue tops, Scot called out, "Coach! We don't have enough backs!"

Seeing that only Bruce stood next to the quarterback, the coach waved irritably at the reserves. "Here's the chance you've been waiting for to step in and get some playing time. We've got two running back spots to fill today. Who wants 'em?"

The ranks of the substitutes had thinned out considerably since the first weeks of practice, and not all of it could be blamed on the flu. Many guys had quit altogether rather than stand around. Only one blue-helmeted player stepped out of the line to join Scot and

35

Bruce.

Coach Ray turned to Bronc, rubbing the stubble on his cheeks in amazement. "Bronc, don't we have any more backs? You mean the rest are all linemen?"

"If they're not, we've got the shyest backs in history," Bronc said. "But you know, some of the guys on defense used to work out with the backs."

Coach Ray scanned the defense, searching for the smaller, quicker players. Chip lowered his head, hoping to avoid the coach's search. But he had a feeling he was going to be chosen. Maybe it was because the coach liked saying his name, or what he believed to be his name.

"Demorg! How would you like to play right halfback?"

He felt as if he'd just been identified out of a police lineup of criminals. *Great,* he thought. *Another chance to make a fool out of myself.* Eric's shrill laugh didn't help matters.

"You can't do that, coach!" pleaded P.C. "You're breaking up this fine defensive machine on the left side."

"Do you mind?" sighed Coach Ray. "I need a back for this scrimmage."

P.C. hung an arm across Chip's shoulder. "Tough break, kid," he teased. "They finally get someone easy to tackle in the backfield, and you get switched out of the defense."

Dan winked at him and said, "You're still getting over the flu, right? Do me a favor and breathe on Roosevelt during the huddle."

"Sure thing," smiled Chip. "I guess our defensive contest is off for today."

"Are you kidding?" squawked P.C. "With you out of the way, we'll finally have a fighting chance. Do you realize we've given up forty-five more yards than the other side, even with our handicap?"

36

As Chip drew near the offensive huddle, he was awkwardly aware that the entire group was staring at him. Most seemed suspicious of the new runner.

"Sorry, you can't join the team," said Scot seriously. "Not when you're dressed like that."

Chip blushed as he looked down at his running shoes. He had always been self-conscious that he didn't have real football shoes like many of the players. But then Bruce snapped the elastic of his vest, and Chip realized he was still wearing the blue top of the defense. They were still snickering about that when Coach Ray poked his head into the huddle. From the way the coach rubbed his hands and grinned secretively, Chip could tell how much he enjoyed calling plays.

"This is the real thing now, boys. Any penalties will be called and marked off. Now listen up. Our first play will be 31 Red, on two. Let's go!"

Chip's clap came so late that it was only a small echo of the others. But the clapping didn't worry him; he was desperately fighting off a feeling of utter panic. What in the world did "31 Red" mean? He lined up an arm's length to the right of Bruce, searching the offensive formation for some clue as to what would happen. Although it was a cool, late-summer afternoon and he hadn't run a step yet, the foam padding of his helmet felt slippery with sweat. *How come they all know what the play is and I don't?* he thought.

P.C. was jumping and waving off to Chip's right, trying to draw his attention. Chip was dimly aware of the motion, but was so frazzled that he didn't even recognize him. Following the others in the three-point stance, he stared at Scot, who had started to shout out numbers.

Not me, not me! Chip pleaded silently. *Give it to someone else!*

But when Scot called out "Two," and the wall of blockers surged into action, Chip saw the quarterback directing the ball straight for his stomach. With a deep breath, Chip opened his arms to take the ball. What he would do once he got it, he had no idea.

At the last instant, Scot slapped the football into Bruce's stomach. Relieved, but still feeling out of place, Chip shuffled after the fullback as he ran into the line of blockers. Chip was still standing, untouched, when the runner was dragged down after a four-yard gain.

"How does it feel to be a star?" It was Dan grinning at him from flat on his back.

"Come on, can't you tell?" he whispered. "I don't know the first thing about what I'm doing."

"What do you mean?" said Dan, removing his protective mouthpiece. Suddenly he nodded. "That's right, you weren't here the day we went over the numbering for the plays. Let's see," he squinted at the other fallen bodies sorting themselves out. After retracing the path Bruce had run he said, "That must have been a 31 Red. Lucky for you! You were just a decoy."

Dan scrambled to his feet and caught Bruce by the elbow. After a whispered exchange, Bruce stared at Chip with wide eyes. "Are you kidding? He was fakin' it, and didn't know what the play was?" He laughed and poked Dan. "Hey, what if coach had called a forty play, huh?" Chip trailed the fullback to the huddle. "Tell you what," said Bruce over his shoulder. There's no time to go over the plays now, so I guess I'll have to tell you what to do on each play."

"Yeah, thanks," said Chip, his racing heart finally pulling back into his chest where it belonged.

"Fake 44, run 26 White, on three. Go!"

Bruce and Chip shuffled to the backfield positions together. "You're supposed to run over there. Oops! What am I doing, pointing?" Bruce dropped his hand in disgust and muttered, with his eyes fixed on the

38

ground, "Scot comes to the right side and he's going to fake a handoff to you. You run between the right tackle and right end, just like you have the ball."

Chip nodded. "Then what about—"

"Don't worry about the rest; we don't have time," said Bruce. "Just worry about yourself and try not to mess up."

As Bruce had explained, Scot took the ball and veered to the right side. Chip ran forward, brushing past the quarterback, and looked for an opening to the right of Roosevelt. The area was clear and Chip found himself running free past the line of scrimmage. As an afterthought, he wondered if he shouldn't try to block someone. But by the time he located a blue jersey, the whistle had blown and the play had been stopped for no gain. Worse yet, the kid who had taken over his linebacker spot was the last to climb off the runner. It hurt to see P.C. give the boy an enthusiastic pounding on the back.

"Demorg!" shouted the coach. Chip cringed. Now what? "You have to hit that hole faster. Why bother to put a fake in the play if no one believes you have the ball?"

Chip stood awkwardly in the backfield as the offense tried one of their few pass plays on third down. But it fell incomplete. "Three points for the defense," growled Coach Ray. Chip saw P.C. and Dan slap each other's hands with glee. There seemed to be no doubt about it; with Chip switched over to the offense, the defense was playing better. Wiping his forehead, Chip called himself a few more names.

Bruce tugged off his helmet during the short break in the practice and signaled for Chip to join him. The fullback was breathing heavily, adding another load of guilt to the pile Chip already carried. The rest of the offense had been working hard, and Chip hadn't even touched anyone yet.

39

"Listen," said Bruce. "I can't concentrate on what I'm doing when I have to worry about you. So, quick, here's the system. It's easy. No matter what the play is, the system is the same. The first number is the ball carrier, see? Quarterback is 1, left halfback is 2, fullback is 3, right half is 4. The second number is the hole you run to. Anything to the right of the center is even, plays to the left are odd. So between the center and right guard is the 0 hole, between right guard and right tackle is the 2 hole, and so on. The 1 hole is between center and left guard, and so on. Got it? So a 25 play means what?"

Chip thought hard, trying to imagine the blockers at their positions.

"Um, the left halfback carries the ball, and he goes between the left tackle and the left end?"

"See, I told you it was easy," said Bruce. "Now the only other thing is the blocking code. The colors tell you how the backs block on the play. Red means the backs don't block; instead you fake it around end. White means the back nearest the hole leads the blocking through the hole. Blue means *both* blocking backs hit the hole before the runner. Got it?"

Before Chip could answer, Coach Ray ordered practice resumed. From the bark in his voice, the players could tell he was upset with the offense. No one said a word in the huddle. Chip gulped as the coach stared straight at him and snapped, "42 Red, on four!"

"You know the last number means the number the play starts on, don't you?" whispered Bruce.

"Yeah," Chip answered. He wished Bruce hadn't spoken and broken his concentration. Now that he knew he was actually going to run with the ball, he wanted to double-check in his mind where he was supposed to go. The system took some getting used to.

"Hut-one! Hut-two!" shouted Scot as he looked over the defense. Chip bit his lip and rocked forward on his toes. He was tired of being told that he didn't hit the hole fast enough. This time he was going to take off a fraction of a second before he was supposed to. "Hut-three! Hut-" Chip charged ahead just as the center hiked the ball. With one arm held high over his chest and the other low, he ran for the narrow opening between the center and right guard. Somehow, though, he smacked into Scot's shoulder. Dazed, he groped for the ball, but it slid out of his grip as he fell sideways. Luckily, Bruce saw what had happened and pounced on the ball just before two blue-shirted players arrived.

Scot coughed nervously and retreated to the huddle. This time Coach Ray said nothing, but the way he flung down his clipboard and glared with his hands on hips delivered his message perfectly. Before the coach stormed into the huddle, Scot gave Chip a puzzled look. "You came in a little close on that one, didn't you?"

Me! thought Chip. Scot's sloppy handoff had ruined his first run, and given him a scrape on the chin besides. And here Scot was trying to pin it on him! Suddenly, Chip's face flushed as he realized what had happened. The "2" hole was not between the center and guard—it was the guard-tackle slot. He had forgotten that the even numbers in the series started with zero and not two. No wonder he had bumped into Scot! And from the way Bruce was clearing his throat and shaking his head at him, Chip guessed that the fullback knew exactly what had gone on.

"I thought you said you were catching on to this!" said Bruce as they lined up for a 30 White play.

Chip nodded. He was supposed to be the lead blocker on this play. Still shaking with embarrassment from the last play, he didn't notice until he ran past the center that his blocking assignment was Eric! Seeing his enemy rush up to make the tackle, Chip lowered his

41

head and braced himself for a jarring collision. But Eric was able to sidestep most of the block. "Get out of my way, you twerp!" he sneered as he pushed past Chip and lunged at Bruce. Chip's weak block must have helped some, though, because Bruce had gained seven yards by the time Eric wrestled him down. Still, he had to admit he should have done much better.

It wasn't until six plays later that Chip finally got his hands on the football. There was no path through the line, only a pile of bodies. But Chip plowed determinedly ahead for a yard or two before the massive weight of players pinned him to the ground. Wedged so tightly that he could not move until two or three layers of defenders got off, he could see Bruce looking down at him.

"You got a couple of tough yards," said Bruce.

Those few words changed the game of football for Chip from drudgery into an action-packed adventure. He wriggled to his feet and tossed the ball to Bronc, who was marking the forward progress. He knew that he hadn't done anything spectacular, but still he felt proud. He had carried the ball and won approval from one of the team's stars.

As he went out to block on the next play, he noticed for the first time how much he had learned in his weeks of practice. The plays no longer seemed like a confused scramble. As the patterns of play began to come into focus, he no longer had to rely on instinct and reactions. He could see where the tacklers were coming from, and where he had to be to block them out of the way. Of course, his blocking needed improvement. P.C. hopped over him, untouched, to make a tackle on one play. But rather than retreat silently to his huddle, Chip pointed accusingly at the cornerback and grinned. "I'd like to see you try that again!"

P.C. grinned back at him. "You liked that move, huh? Hey, do us a favor and warn us when the play's coming this way. We're still thirty-four yards behind the right side in our contest."

Two plays later, Coach Ray called for 41 Blue. By this time, Chip was able to decode the call in time to think about the path he would take. With a chill, he realized that he would be heading straight into Eric's territory. *I hope somebody blocks him,* he thought.

Chip waited for the other two backs to lead the way, then took the handoff from Scot. There was no mistaking the hole this time! No defensive player was within reach of him as he bolted through a large gap in the line. Bruce then knocked one of the safeties off his feet, leaving a clear field ahead.

Suddenly someone slammed into him from the side and put a bear hug on him. With one arm on the ground to steady himself, Chip somehow kept his balance and tried to twist out of the tackler's arms. As he turned, he found himself helmet to helmet with Eric. The sneer was gone as Eric stared straight into Chip's eyes. With a last bit of effort, Chip broke free from the grip and staggered backwards. A desperate swipe from Eric's arm caused Chip to stumble, but he lurched forward for eight more yards before being tackled from behind.

"Nice run!" shouted Bruce, sounding as much surprised as excited. Eric still stood where Chip had left him, holding out his arms and gaping at Chip as if the runner had passed right through his body.

As Chip filled his slot in the huddle, he could barely keep from shouting with joy as both Scot and Coach Ray offered their hands. The offense was on the move now! Chip could feel the energy in the huddle. Clapping twice as loudly as before, he dashed back to his position.

Fake 40 White, Run 27, Chip repeated to himself. He followed Bruce straight ahead and fell over one of his own blockers. Immediately, he craned his neck to

43

see what was going on around the left end. The defense had fallen for the fake. Even the cornerbacks had rushed up to help plug the middle. The left halfback, running down the left sideline, was twenty yards past the line of scrimmage before many of the defenders even realized he had the ball.

"Ha! Faked you guys out of your pants!" laughed Bruce, elbowing Dan in the stomach.

When practice ended a half hour later, the offense claimed a 24-6 win. They walked off the field with just enough strength left to let loose a few howls and cheers. Chip decided he had never had so much fun in his life. He was walking off the field with the team's best player, or at least very close to him, and star players didn't walk off the field with nerds. Better yet, Eric Youngquist was limping off by himself.

Just before he reached his bike, he waved to Bruce, then turned to see what P.C. had to say this time. "Hey, thanks for running that sixty-yard touchdown to the other side," said the little cornerback. "That turned everything around. Now we have a twenty-yard lead in the great defensive race!"

"Don't thank me," said Chip. "I didn't call the play, and I didn't carry the ball on that one, either."

Dan trudged over very slowly after his day's battle with Roosevelt. "Now when you come back to linebacker we'll at least have a little cushion. It'll probably take you a good two practices to help us blow our lead."

"Forget the linebacker stuff," said Chip casually, spinning the combination lock on his bike. "It's fun being a back. You know, that Bruce is really a great guy."

4
The Punt that Got Away

"Chip Demory?" Rennie searched Bruce's face to see if his fellow running back was putting him on. When he saw that Bruce was serious, he burst into laughter. "Are you kidding? *He* took *my* place?" The peals of laughter cut deeply into Chip's pride, far deeper than Eric's remarks ever had. Eric laughed out of obvious spite, but Rennie had no such motive. He truly could not help himself, even though Chip was sitting well within listening range. Evidently the thought of Chip filling his shoes for a practice struck him as ridiculous.

Rennie had washed away all the confidence that Chip had so painfully earned in the scrimmage. But, just as suddenly, Bruce retrieved it. "Don't laugh," he said. "He did a good job."

As far as Chip was concerned, Bruce had just made a

friend for life. Rennie shrugged and trotted off to play catch with Scot. Chip tried hard to forgive Rennie's thoughtlessness. Who could blame Rennie for being surprised? Chip hadn't done much before to prove he could play.

Most of the team was lying against the brick wall of the school, where the shade had protected the last stand of lush grass from drying out like the rest of the field. Despite their lounging, very few actually seemed relaxed. In one hour the team from Monroe School would be there for the first game of the year. Coach Ray had done nothing to ease the tension in his players. He had been maddeningly secretive about what would happen, who would start, and how many reserves might play.

Those unsolved questions made it difficult for Chip to get comfortable. His legs refused to stay in one spot, and his stomach felt like it was turning upside down. He supposed that he probably should have had supper before the game. But even if his mom had been home in time to make him something, he wasn't sure he could have eaten it.

His new friend Bruce, however, seemed cool about it all. With his arms folded across his chest and his eyes shut, he almost seemed in danger of falling asleep. Chip tried to will himself to act that calmly, but then got twice as jumpy as before when he saw the school custodian plant red flags in the corners of the chalked end zones.

Stretching out his legs again, Chip noticed how clean his mom had gotten his practice uniform. "How come the coach waits until now to give the game jerseys?" he asked Bruce.

"Tradition, I guess," Bruce answered without lifting an eyelid. He yawned, then added, "He always waits till now. It's part of his pregame pep job. He likes everyone tense and psyched up."

Chip found himself yawning, too, though he was far

46

from tired. He ached to ask Bruce what he thought his chances were of getting in at running back. Everyone knew he had done well at practice, he thought. Maybe he and Rennie could alternate and carry instructions from the bench to the huddle.

Even Bruce sat up at the sound of the van as it arrived. Coach Ray hopped out one door, dressed in a sport jacket and tie, and pulled open the side door. Bronc, in a blue sweater with the sleeves rolled up, followed him and helped him carry in the boxes. Without a word or a whistle from the coaches, the team followed them into the school to the locker room.

What a change three weeks can make! thought Chip. Nothing in the room seemed remotely scary now. He was able to walk right into the middle of the group and find a spot on the concrete floor reserved for him by Dan and P.C.

"This doesn't mean it's permanent," said Coach Ray, waving his clipboard, "but this is the starting offensive lineup for the game. Come and get your game jersey when I call your name. The tackles are Baxter and Ellingsly."

Chip had to scrunch against the bench to help give the two a path to the front. They claimed their extra-large jerseys and held them up by a corner, as if afraid to wrinkle them. Midnight blue with white numerals, the jerseys looked professional.

"How do they assign numbers?" Chip asked.

"It's the usual pattern," Dan answered. "Quarterbacks are teens, runners twenties and thirties, defensive backs forties, linebackers and centers fifties, guards sixties, tackles seventies, ends eighties. Nineties are for subs."

Chip could not keep his eyes off the emptying box as the rest of the starting linemen came forward. This was his first game, he kept reminding himself. Now that he knew he was better than anyone had suspected, he

47

pictured himself scoring a long touchdown in that sharp uniform.

"Wilkes, Schultz," called out the coach. When they returned, Chip saw Bronc pull out a number 20. *Wouldn't it be great if that were mine?* thought Chip. *Why not? Bruce says I was great.*

"Ruiz!"

Jolted back to reality, Chip felt foolish. *How dumb could I be to think I might beat out Rennie? Rennie can run twice as fast as I can.*

"All of these players will also start on defense," announced the coach, "with two exceptions."

Amid a chorus of excited whispers, Chip felt a nudge from behind.

"Hey, this could get interesting," winked P.C. When Bronc pulled out a large number 83, P.C. leaned over to Dan. "You might get lucky. That's a lineman's number."

"Atkinson," said Coach Ray, and P.C. pounded Dan on the back.

Dan made no move to get up, though. "Which Atkinson?" asked several voices.

"The one who plays right end."

"The lucky bum," sighed Dan as his brother hurried forward. No sooner had he grabbed his jersey and sat down than both Dan and P.C. poked Chip. Chip then saw a number 55 displayed in Bronc's hands. A linebacker's number!

Please, let me have that one! Chip pleaded silently.

"Youngquist." There was an extra swagger to his walk as Eric proudly strode forward to claim his starting position. Chip rolled his eyes in disgust. "What a joke!" he muttered. "He can't tackle. I ran right through his arms in that scrimmage."

"What did I tell you?" whispered Dan. "Now that he's in, he'll leave you alone."

As the rest of the names were called, Chip clung to

the hope of a reserve running back spot. He *must* have impressed them; Bruce had as much as said so. It was all right with him if he only got in for a few plays. He would show them what he could do.

"Demorg!" Nearly stepping on a few legs in his eagerness, Chip made his way to the front. The jersey Bronc held was rumpled, but Chip thought he could make out a number 37: a running back number! He grinned at Bruce and snatched the jersey, then held it out to get a better look. Fifty-seven! Chip hardly noticed the shoves from others trying to get past him to pick up their tops. The roller coaster of emotions he had been riding had just thrown him off at the bottom.

As he trudged back to his spot on the floor, the sounds of the bantering among the players seemed miles away.

"I hear football players wear their IQs on their jerseys," Dan was explaining, holding up his 99. "That makes me the smartest one here."

"Forty-six!" groaned P.C. "What a blah number! Name one great player who ever wore 46. Name just one."

Ignoring them, Chip glared down at his number 57. It was depressing how a number could ruin a perfectly good jersey.

"Hey, Chip!"

Chip swung his head around and, as if their heads were all connected by strings, half the players on the sidelines turned to look. Chip's surprise turned to anger when he saw that it was Tom grinning and waving at him. The disappointment of being demoted to reserve linebacker had put him in a grouchy mood to begin with. Throughout the first half of the game he had stared sullenly at the proceedings on the field. Some of the others had yelled encouragement to the starters, but Chip couldn't get into that. It especially

49

grated on him to see Eric playing defense. Eric was playing the middle linebacker spot like a big shot, clapping and yelling warnings to his teammates, and jumping in the air after making a tackle. The coaches hadn't even looked at any of the reserves so far. And now there was Tom calling out to him, with that silly, homemade haircut and goofy grin.

What is he doing here? Chip wondered. *So what if he's a good friend; he doesn't belong here.* Tom couldn't have told if the Green Bay Packers were a football team or a labor union. A lot of boys thought of him as a wimp. It wasn't really fair: Tom just didn't happen to care about sports. He was a nice guy and a good friend, but Chip wished he would act a little more normal.

"What are you doing here?" Chip asked, so quietly that Tom barely heard.

"Come on, I came to watch the star in action," said Tom.

Eric, who was pacing the sidelines while the offense was on the field, overheard. "You told him you're the big star?" he laughed. "Then what are you doin' on the bench the whole game?" Several boys joined in on the chuckling.

"Shut up," said Chip, glaring at both Eric and Tom. Just then, a long pass from Scott to Andy regained the team's attention. Chip slipped away and led Tom far from the action, behind a row of parents watching from behind the bench. Chip judged from their lack of enthusiasm that many of them were parents of scrubs.

"What are you doing here?" Chip asked.

"I already told you—"

"I'm not the star," snapped Chip. "I never said I was."

"But you—"

"I said I did well in *one* practice. That's all. Now I'm on the bench. I haven't played all game."

"I'm sorry," said Tom, with his head down and

50

hands stuck in his pockets. "I just thought I'd come and root for you." Peeking through the row of parents, he asked, "Why was Eric Youngquist being so mean?"

"Because that's the way scum like him always act," Chip spat.

"I don't know him that well," shrugged Tom. "But I don't remember him being so bad when he was in my Sunday school class a few years back."

"Eric goes to our church?" asked Chip, suspiciously. "How come I never see him?" He couldn't imagine why God would want anything to do with someone like Eric. The thought of Eric in church made him uncomfortable, an intrusion on another part of his life.

"I don't know," answered Tom. "It's a big church. Maybe he goes in the middle of the week. Maybe he doesn't go at all now."

"That's more likely," nodded Chip. "If I acted the way he did, I wouldn't have the guts to step inside a church."

"We should get back to the game, shouldn't we?" asked Tom. "You might be called on to go in." Seeing Chip roll his eyes, he said, "Well, aren't you even interested in who's winning?"

Chip turned his back on the field. "Is that a good enough answer for you? This whole thing has been a big pain since the first day. It probably wouldn't be so bad if there weren't creeps like Eric around to spoil it for everyone." He paused as if coming to an important decision. "I'll probably stick it out for this year. But next year, I'm going out for soccer. Jason says it's fun most of the time. Hey, why don't you come out for it, too? The three of us could have a great time."

"Naw," said Tom, kicking a stone loose from the ground. "I'm no good at that." Then, brightening, he said, "I know one thing we can all do together next year. We'll be in the youth group at church. My brother goes to it all the time, and he says it's a blast."

51

"Yeah?" said Chip. "I'm not sure." The idea didn't sound the best to him. He was already working under a social handicap with Tom as a friend. If he was in a church group, too, well, everybody would think he was really out of it. He didn't think God would mind. What good would it do God if Chip lost friends over something like that? "Trouble is, they probably pick on the little guys. It might be better to wait until we aren't the youngest in the group."

"Come on," laughed Tom. "This is a church. What are they going to do, mug you and dump you off in a dark alley?"

"Very funny," said Chip. He heard Coach Ray's booming voice ordering the defense back on the field. The offense must have been stopped again. There was Eric strapping on his helmet and sprinting back on the field like a madman. "Hey, Tom. Do they let anyone join? The youth group, I mean."

"Well, I think you would have to belong to the church."

Frowning, Chip went on. "You don't suppose Eric would join."

"Eric who?" Then, following Chip's gaze, he said, "I don't know."

"I'll tell you one thing, if Eric joins that group, I wouldn't come near it if you paid me!"

Tom whistled. "Boy, the guy must be pretty bad!"

"You wouldn't believe him. I'd stay away from him if I were you."

"Relax," said Tom. "If he doesn't do much in church now, he's not likely to join then."

"Demorg!"

Although the voice barely filtered through the noise of the sideline chatter to his ears, Chip jumped. When he heard it again, louder and more urgent, he wheeled and dashed back to the bench.

"What are you doing? That's not your name," said

Tom, but Chip was in too big a hurry to explain.

"Demorg, for cryin' out loud, where are you?" Coach Ray was saying when Chip reached the sidelines. Forcing his way through a cluster of players, he reported to the coach.

"Where have you been?" demanded the coach. Without waiting for an answer, he shoved him toward the field. "Ruiz has the wind knocked out of him. Take over at left linebacker!"

"Go get 'em, Chip!" yelled P.C.

Chip didn't know how many more shocks his system could take in one day. The switch from total boredom and hopelessness to a supercharged high in just twenty seconds had him dizzy. He raced onto the field about two steps faster than he had ever run in his life. The Forest Grove defense didn't bother with huddles, so he headed straight for his position. Eric happened to step backward into his path, and he brushed lightly against him. *Oh, no,* thought Chip, poised for another confrontation. But the middle linebacker seemed lost in his own thoughts, and barely recognized that a new player was in the game.

In fact, none of his teammates seemed to have noticed his arrival. Chip was used to P.C.'s constant chatter between plays, and Dan always had some comment, even if he just groaned. Chip felt as though he were an intruder in the silent wave of blue shirts.

It didn't help matters that he had been ignoring the game. Chip had no idea what down it was, or how many yards there were to go. He wasn't even sure of the score, although his team had been ahead, 13-6, the last time he checked. But as the green and white Monroe team lined up, he began to feel more sure of himself. For one thing, it gave him a huge shot of confidence to see Roosevelt Baxter crouching a few feet away on the left side of the line. Better yet, the Monroe players, even the linemen, weren't very big.

53

This is a real game, Chip kept reminding himself as the Monroe quarterback gave out signals. They tried a running play up the middle, but the smallish blockers could not make a dent in the Forest Grove line. Five Forest Grove players had already wrapped up the little back and were driving him back when Chip arrived. Just to be in on the action, he pushed along with the rest of the tacklers until the whistle blew.

This is lots easier than stopping our own offense, thought Chip. For the first time in his life, he felt like a real athlete. It was such a feeling of power that he could almost forgive Eric for strutting around all game. Having easily brushed aside his blocker the play before, Chip hoped they would run a play to his side. He could see himself storming into the backfield to wreck the play before it started.

Roosevelt seemed to be waving him forward. Chip ran up, wondering what the star lineman had to say. But Roosevelt said nothing as he dug his cleats into the ground. Confused, Chip looked around and saw Bruce backpedaling all by himself. A quick look at the Monroe formation confirmed that this was going to be a punt. No wonder Roosevelt motioned him forward; they were all supposed to be on the line to try to block the kick!

Chip relaxed as he imitated the lineman's stance. He had never practiced rushing a punter, but he knew what would happen. No one ever blocked a punt; you just went through the motions, pushing and shoving a little until the punter kicked it away.

What he couldn't figure out was why there wasn't a Monroe blocker in front of him. There didn't seem to be anyone between him and the punter. When something didn't make sense, Chip usually suspected that he was doing something wrong.

Am I in the wrong spot? he wondered. *But where else can I go?* Chip finally shrugged, figuring some Monroe

54

player would show up to block him. They must know what they were doing.

When the ball was hiked, Chip ran forward. To his amazement, no Monroe player showed the slightest interest in him. Chip was so startled that he slowed up. What was going on? It couldn't be a fake punt, because he saw the punter right in front of him step forward to gain momentum for his punt. Chip was close enough so that, with a quick spurt, he could easily smother the kick. But he had never seen it done or prepared himself for just *how* to do it. Were you suppose to hold out your hands, or run into the kicker? And how did you keep from getting kicked in the stomach?

The questions paralyzed him so that he had stopped moving altogether by the time the punt sailed away. Chip watched it bounce out-of-bounds, which saved him the trouble of blocking for the kick return.

As he stood there watching the punter walk off, it suddenly hit him how stupid he had been. A Monroe player had blown his blocking assignment. If Chip had been at all alert, he would have taken advantage of it. As it was, he had had to work hard to *stop* himself from tackling the kicker before the ball had even dropped! On the second play of his career, he had been given a great chance to be a star, and he had been too timid to accept it.

His eyes shot quickly to the bench. Had anyone noticed? The players milling around the field didn't even look his way; they must have been too busy with their own assignments. But a dreaded tap on the shoulder convinced Chip that Coach Ray had detected the error. A substitute had come in to take his place.

Chip was certain the coach had seen it all. The man didn't look at Chip for the rest of the game. Chip's substitute stayed in the game even when Forest Grove went back on defense. *Too chicken to block a kick,* thought Chip. *I won't get another chance to play for the rest of the year!*

Forest Grove wore down the smaller Monroe team for another touchdown in the final period. The referee shot off a gun to signal the end of the game, and Forest Grove danced off the field celebrating a 19-7 win.

"Way to go, Chip!" shouted Tom, above the uproar. That crazy Tom seemed more excited about the win than most of the players.

"Yeah, way to go, star! " said Eric. Chip saw Eric's uniform, coated with smudges of dirt, and looked down at his own spotless pants. Although he had done almost nothing for the past four hours, he felt as though he barely had the strength to walk the three blocks to his home. His anger had faded. He couldn't blame Tom, or Eric, either. He felt totally defeated. And he didn't care if he ever got another chance to play. *A loser like me would probably just blow it again, anyway,* he concluded.

5
Trumpet Call

The long line of cars waiting to pull into the senior high school parking lot were starting to tie up traffic on Princeton Avenue. From their spot at the end of the line, the Demorys could see their prospects of finding a parking place in the school's cramped lot were poor.

"You can tell this is a game of unbeaten teams," said Mr. Demory, his eyes darting, looking for a spot on the street. "Last time I came to one of Jill's games, you could have camped out in that lot and never been disturbed."

Chip scanned his side of the street. Just behind them, a turn signal blinked as a driver prepared to pull away from the curb. "There's one opening up behind you, Dad."

"Come on, fella, move it," said Mr. Demory. The car edged out of the spot and went around them. Seeing that no one had come up behind them yet, Mr. Demory backed up and moved into the spot. "I was wondering when he was going to wake up. I paid him a fortune to sit there and reserve that place for me."

"Really? How much did you have to pay?" asked Tom.

Chip groaned. "Come on, Tom, can't you tell he's teasing?"

"Lock up, men," said Mr. Demory. "Glad you could come along tonight, Tom. I didn't know you were a sports buff."

"Well, I'm not really," grinned Tom. "But Chip's football game was kind of interesting, so I figured this might be, too. Besides," he said, patting his black instrument case, "I think this'll be a riot with my trumpet along. Maybe I can add some excitement to the game."

"You're crazy!" said Chip, hurrying to keep up with his dad's pace. "Why did you bring that thing, anyway?"

"Chip's right," said Mr. Demory over his shoulder. "I'm not sure they'll let you bring that into the gym. You'd better talk to the coach about it."

While Tom sought out the volleyball coach, Chip and his dad headed into the stands. The movable bleachers seemed to wobble with each step, no matter how lightly they walked. Finding a spot halfway up, they sat back and watched Jill warm up. The team didn't have any official warm-up suits, and Jill stood out in the sky blue one Dad had bought her for her birthday. During the spiking drill, she crouched and then floated high in the air. Chip wished he could jump that high. At the top of her leap, she drilled the ball across the net—but it landed beyond the end line of the other court. Frowning, she swung both arms like windmills to get them loose.

The Demorys had room enough to put their feet on the seats below and to lean back on the ones behind.

Still, the gymnasium was almost half full on the home side, far different from the last time they had come. "A little success really brings people out," commented Dad. "We're ranked third, and East is fourth in the state coaches' poll." Chip hadn't ever heard of a state ranking for high school girls' volleyball. But, knowing how his dad combed the sports pages, he didn't doubt the statement.

Even if they hadn't seen Tom run up the steps toward them, they would have heard him coming. *Clomp! Clomp!* Chip thought the bleachers were going to collapse. "Hey! The coach, Mrs. Campbell, thought it would be a great idea!" Tom spouted. "The more noise, the better. Know what else? She asked me if I wanted to play the national anthem before the game. Usually they use a record."

Watching Jill muff an attempted setup, Dad said, "Well, bugler, do you happen to know reveille? I don't think Jill is awake yet."

"Sure, that's easy," answered Tom, putting the mouthpiece to his lips.

Chip pulled the instrument away from him. "When are you going to stop being so gullible?" he asked, shaking his head. "Dad's only kidding." A group of girls were standing in the aisle, shielding the clock from his sight, so Chip leaned across his dad's lap to check his watch. Three minutes until playing time.

Chip was watching the trickle of latecomers on the home side when he spotted two familiar faces. Bruce and Scot made their way into the gym and stood in the entrance for a moment. With their curly hair, jeans, and matching baseball league Windbreakers, they looked almost like twins from a distance. Scot shrugged and followed Bruce to a first-row seat near the door.

Those two were like a harsh light that exposed the blemish sitting on Chip's left. Until that moment, he

59

had been happy to have Tom along. But he had never dreamed that some of the best players on the football team would be at the game. It was bad enough if they saw him sitting with his dad, but what would they think if they saw Tom with him again? Chip was especially worried about Bruce. The guy had been nice to him since that day he filled in for Rennie. If Chip had any chance left of getting important people to notice him, Bruce was his best bet. But Bruce was probably already going out on a limb just by talking to him. *He wouldn't come near anyone like Tom,* thought Chip. *If Bruce sees us sitting together, he'll really wonder about me.*

Well, at least there are a lot of people tonight, he thought, looking at the crowd. *They aren't going to notice me.* Just to be safe, though, he leaned back in his seat so that his dad's shoulder would block his face from their view.

Then he saw Tom with his horn up, waiting for a signal. East had already assembled on the sidelines, and Mrs. Campbell had just ended the drills for her squad. *If he blows that thing, everyone in the place will be looking at us,* he thought.

"You're not going to play the national anthem up here, are you?" Chip asked quickly.

"Why not? They'll all be able to hear just fine."

"But wouldn't it be more, uh, proper to have you standing out on the floor?"

"Not a bad idea," said his dad.

"OK. Wish me luck." Tom grinned as he pounded back down the steps. Chip had to admit he played well. He didn't waver on a single note. While some of the crowd near them joined in singing, Chip's mind was working feverishly. He had just barely dodged this catastrophe. But Tom was planning to use that crazy horn the whole game. Bruce and Scot couldn't help but notice Tom; Chip had to make sure that when they did,

60

he was out of the picture.

"Well played, bugler," said Dad when Tom returned. "What do you plan to do for an encore?"

Grinning and brushing back his jaggedly cut hair, Tom blasted a brief familiar sports tune. "Charge!" yelled most of the home team spectators in response. Seeing that practically everyone in the place was turning to look at them, Chip quickly let his jacket slip down through an opening in the bleachers. Dropping down after it, he said, "Oops. Dropped my jacket. Be right back." It was an easy climb down the ironworks supporting the collapsible bleachers. There were already a few candy wrappers and popcorn containers littering the floor next to his jacket. It was a fine excuse to kill a little more time, and Chip collected as many as he could in one armful. Dumping them into the trash can by the wall, he returned and tried to locate the section in which he had been sitting. At the same time, he wished for a plan that could get him through the rest of the game.

"Hey! What's taking you?" Tom's head was poking through directly above him.

"There was a bunch of garbage down here, so I picked some of it up." Climbing back up through the supporting works, he had to admit he was beaten. With Tom carrying on, Bruce would notice him for sure—unless the games were so exciting that no one paid attention to that stupid trumpet.

Unfortunately, the first game dragged on with neither side scoring well on their serves. Chip spent most of it watching the two heads in the first row, and leaning back whenever it seemed one of them was turning around. *If Tom plays that 'Charge' thing again, I'll scream,* he thought. But of course, Tom kept at it. All Chip could do was try to make himself as small as possible. From what he saw of the game, Jill was playing well. That got his normally quiet dad talking nonstop. He always did when he got excited at one of Jill's games.

After Jill's team finally won the first game, Tom sprang another surprise. "How about a little intermission entertainment?"

Resisting the urge to slug his friend, Chip got up and walked down three rows before turning to his dad. "Want something to drink from the concessions?"

"Not for me, thanks," Dad said, prying a dollar out of his wallet. "I get so wrapped up in these games, I'd probably just spill the whole thing. But the bugler's probably running pretty dry. Get something for the two of you."

Tom was into his first number before Chip snatched away the dollar. Chip sighed heavily after yet another narrow escape. He started cutting straight across the bleachers to avoid running into Bruce and Scot. But when he checked on them again, he found their seats empty. *Maybe they left,* Chip hoped as he bounced down to the floor. Somehow, though, he still didn't feel that terrific. Even in his narrow escapes, something was gnawing at him. His feelings of guilt were harder to escape.

He stepped straight from the sounds of Tom's trumpet into the smoke of the lobby. It was always the same at these events. No matter how small the crowd, the smoke was still penetrating. Chip glided through the clusters of people, pretending he was a running back dodging open-field tacklers. No one so much as touched him by the time he reached the concession stand.

There was nothing there resembling a line. People jockeyed for position and tried to catch the attendant's eye before someone else did. Moving quickly into a vacated slot, Chip discovered Bruce just ahead and to the left. The fullback had made it to the counter and was tapping his quarters on it, waiting for his drink to

62

come. At first Chip thought of backing out of line, but the space behind him had already been filled in. He found himself being funneled closer to Bruce, with only one man screening him from view. Chip saw the attendant bring two plastic cups of orange soda pop, then felt a nudge. It was his neighbor, Mr. O'Neill.

"Hi, there, Chip. Your sister's doing a fine job," he said, scratching his beard.

His cover was blown. But Chip saw a way to turn it to his advantage. Pretending he hadn't seen Bruce, he announced loudly, "Oh, Jill's doing all right, I guess. But I think she'll really get going in the second game. It always takes her awhile to warm up, you know."

Bruce took a long sip and turned to Chip on his way out. Without any greeting he said, "So that's your sister out there, huh? Number 15?"

"Yep," said Chip, acting as matter-of-factly as he knew how.

Bruce nodded. "We're taking off. Their games take too long. Scot and I are going over to the arcade before it closes."

It all worked out after all, thought Chip as Bruce pushed past. *They have to be impressed that I'm Jill's brother, especially after the way she played.*

Suddenly Bruce stopped and grabbed Chip's shoulder. Chip waited for him to finish swallowing. "You know, you should get your buddy to bring his horn to our games," said Bruce. "The last one we had was so quiet it didn't even seem like a real game."

"He's not really my buddy," Chip found himself explaining. But Bruce and Scot had already moved away and were pushing through the outside doors. *So they saw me with Tom,* Chip thought. *Why does he have to be so weird?* Chip couldn't see any way around it. He was going to have to avoid Tom for a while. At least for the rest of the football season.

When Chip returned to his seat, Tom was making a

63

bigger spectacle of himself than ever, bowing to the applause. The adults seemed to think he was funny, anyway. Chip slumped in his seat, muscles aching from the prolonged tension, and handed Tom his drink. A man several rows ahead of them waved at his dad.

"Hey, Chuck! Your Jill looks good out there!"

"Not only that, but she's playing well, too," laughed Dad. He was beaming, and his chest was swelling as if he were savoring the most delicious moment in his life. Chip had seen that look a few times before, and always when Jill was playing exceptionally well at something. Before this, Chip had always joined in the applause for Jill. But he wasn't feeling at all gracious anymore.

I've never seen him act that way when I *do anything,* he thought, watching his dad's eyes as they followed Jill. *Not likely to, either. Don't you think I try as hard as she does? All Miss Perfect out there has to do is show up and everyone* oohs *and* ahs *over her. I'm just her klutzy brother.* He ignored Tom throughout the second game, and took a morbid delight in how it was turning out. Jill's team fell behind early and lost the game badly.

Chip listened to his dad nervously mumbling unheard advice to Jill's team, and finally turned to Tom. "You mean you aren't going to treat us to another concert?"

Tom's eyes lit up. "Oh, I almost forgot. Any requests?"

But before he could play, Chip pulled him back down to his seat. "That was such a short game they're not even taking a break. See, they're already serving." Bitterness had ruined the evening for him. When the East team scored he grumbled, and when Jill made a good play for her team he sulked about why God had given her all the talent when he needed it worse than she did. When Jill won a round of applause with a

64

diving save of a hard spike, Chip didn't join in.

But as the game went on, even Chip was drawn into its intensity. The teams were so evenly matched and were playing so hard that the spectators began to look as drained as the players. Tom's latest "Charge" number had attracted only a few hoarse cheers.

Tom shrugged and packed away the instrument. "My hands are getting too sweaty to play anyway," he said.

The gymnasium grew quiet when the ball was served. Spectators on each side seemed to be trying to will the ball to hit the ground on the other team's court. Chip's dad was still muttering instructions under his breath, and his clenched fists jerked in spasms, as if he were trying to play the game for Jill.

The tension pulled Chip back to Jill's side. When an East player stood back and let a ball drop near the line, he and a large share of the home crowd started yelling, "That was in!" But the referee refused to be swayed, and awarded the point to East. That put them ahead, 19-18. Two more points and they would win.

East served again, a deep, spinning shot to the corner. A good save by Jill's teammate sent the ball to her spot on the corner of the front row. As Jill wound up her fist and jumped, two East players crowded the net to attempt a block. "Spike it!" gasped Chip. But Jill eased up and tapped the ball down the row, almost directly over the net. Somehow, though, her teammate pounded it straight down into the netting. The muffed spike gave East a 20-18 lead.

"Why didn't she take the spike herself?" complained Chip. "She's the best player out there."

"Now, don't get on your sister for that," his dad whispered back, wiping his palms on his pants. "You see, that's another example of what makes her a good player. Sure, she could have hit it over the net. But it wasn't a good set. Why, she was at least three feet from the net! So she gave it to another girl. Jill doesn't hog the ball even if she could do better herself. That keeps the team playing as a team. See that? She just told the girl who missed not to worry about it. The game's on the line, and she's still a good sport."

All right, already, thought Chip. *You'd think she was a saint.*

A burst of relieved applause and cheering followed a wide serve by the East team. Now it was Jill's turn to serve. The room was so quiet, that Chip could hear the echoing thud as Jill pounded her serves across the net. Three straight points brought the home fans to the edge of their seats as their team took the lead, 21-20. Then Jill hit one final overhand serve that spun crazily away from an East player, beyond reach of her teammates.

The gym exploded in noise, and soon all the girls were hugging each other, even the ones who hadn't played. Chip saw his dad rush down toward the floor, and he and Tom followed at a more cautious pace. By the time they reached the court, a reporter had pushed his way next to Jill. "Everyone on the team works hard," she was saying. "We're all part of this win, 'cause we push each other in practice."

Chip bristled when he heard it. It was almost as if she were aiming her comments at him, insisting that everyone was the same. For a second, guilt washed over him as he thought of how he was considering abandoning Tom to avoid being tagged as a loser. *It's not the same,* he thought, fighting the feeling. *It's easy for her. She's got it all. What's she got to lose by being that way?*

Jill finally made her way over to them. "Hi!" she said, with a bright smile at each of them. "Thanks for coming!"

She's so perfect I could throw up, thought Chip as his dad swung her around in a hug.

6
The Penalty

Chip had not been wrong about that punt play coming back to haunt him. At the next practice, Bronc took him aside and asked, "What's wrong with you, Chip? You were a tiger during that one practice, but you haven't done a thing since." Chip could only shrug, paw the ground with his foot, and promise to try harder.

Worse yet, Coach Ray didn't call his name once during practice, not even to yell at him. He remembered a remark Jill had made once when Dad had complained that a coach was always picking on her. "It's when they don't think you're worth yelling at that you have to worry," she'd said.

When Forest Grove went to the municipal park to play Willow Creek, Chip found himself, as usual, on the wrong side of the white lines. He had been standing and watching so long that his legs were starting to throb. The lights over the field made even the scuffed helmets shine against the black of a moonless night.

The uniforms seemed brighter, the grass greener, the game more real.

But as had happened so often, Chip's thoughts drifted away from the game in front of him. His dad had dropped him off at the field on the way to a meeting. Before he had left, he had completely caught Chip off guard.

"You've got a game next week, too, don't you?" Dad had asked.

"Yeah, cross town over at Brycelin Heights. Tuesday night."

Dad had pulled out that black book that he kept tucked in the inside pocket of his suits. "I'll work on getting it cleared so I can come watch."

"Uh, well, if you've got something better to do . . ." Chip had stammered.

"Think you can get me a good seat?" Dad had said, knowing full well that there weren't any stands at Brycelin Heights.

Chip's first thought had been that his dad would find out for sure next week that he was not good enough to get into a game. For the first two quarters of the game, he moped about his klutziness and his bad luck. But by the third period, a stubborn streak had surfaced in him that refused to accept humiliation in front of his dad. *Somehow I've got to get into the starting lineup,* he thought. Then he laughed at himself for even imagining such a thing. But gradually, the scene before him captured his interest. Each missed tackle or block, each dropped pass, and each penalty gave more proof that the starters weren't perfect.

"Hey, all-star!" Eric jarred his thoughts loose with his shout. The middle linebacker threw back his head to gulp water out of a paper cup, crumpled the cup, and tossed it on the ground. Eric had been getting laughs calling him all-star ever since the last game. Although Chip had vowed many times to get even, he

68

began to see that it was no use. Eric had won the starting role, and at the same time had won their private war. "Wake up, all-star, you gotta be ready to save the game for us."

"Shut your mouth, Youngquist!" said Chip.

"Oh, sure thing! I don't want to get an all-star mad at me."

Dan moved over to Chip, pounding his helmet on his thigh pad. "I guess I blew that call. I really thought Eric would settle down once he made the starting lineup. He must be more insecure than I thought. You know, that's the trouble with making predictions. There's always a chance that you may be wrong."

"Just a chance?" hooted P.C., sitting on his helmet in front of them. "Atkinson, if you predicted the sun would rise tomorrow, I wouldn't bet on it."

Chip was pretty sure of the answer to his own question, but he had to voice it anyway. "Dan, is there any chance of us getting in the game?"

"You're asking me?" said Dan. "I don't want to go out on a limb one way or another. But I haven't seen a substitution all night."

Chip was aware of that, and he knew the reason why. Willow Creek posed a far greater challenge than Monroe had. They were well-coached, fast, strong, and even had one boy who could make Roosevelt work awfully hard. Chip could see the strain on the starters' faces on the rare occasions when they came close to him. Even Bruce hadn't said anything to him at halftime. He had just squinted through the harsh lights at the Willow Creek squad, doubled over with his hands on his hips. Although Forest Grove held an 8-6 lead into the third period, this was serious business.

Rennie found out just how serious it was late in the third period. While trying to fake out one defender, he was hit hard from behind, bounced through the air, and landed on his back. Dazed, he limped off the field.

Seeing his chance, Chip sought out Coach Ray. He stood close enough to the coach to rub shoulders, and even ventured a foot out onto the field, trying to attract the coach's attention. But if Coach Ray did happen to turn his way, he looked right through him. After a time out, Rennie ran back on the field. All the starters were still in.

With nervous energy building up inside of him, Chip pushed his way behind the line of reserves. *Maybe if I do some really hard sprints, I can show them that I'm ready,* he thought. Somehow, the strange lighting and the darkness made him feel as though he were flying as he raced down the sidelines. He pictured himself running into the middle of a packed stadium with an announcer shouting, "At left linebacker, 6 feet, 4 inches, 230 pounds, number 57, Chip Demory!"

As he puffed back toward the bench, Dan reached out and slowed him down with his arm. "What's the matter? Your pants on fire?"

"No," gasped Chip, "just trying to stay ready in case I get in the game."

"Now there's an optimist for you," said Dan.

"I suppose you always keep your wallet open just in case some dollar bills happen to be falling from the sky," added P.C. But Chip thought he saw Bronc give him a quick glance. Just for good measure, he sprinted down the sidelines one more time.

Late in the fourth quarter, however, Chip had conceded that he would not play this game. He hadn't really expected it would be that easy to work himself back into favor with the coaches. In fact, as he watched the furious action on the field, he had a twinge of doubt about even wanting to be out there. Still trailing by two points, Willow Creek had driven deep into Forest Grove territory. Most of their yards came on power plays off tackle. Eric was no longer prancing around and hollering; he had all he could handle battling the opposing center. The Willow Creek center, a stocky guy with his red shirttail always hanging out, seemed to be a tough character. He and Eric were often still wrestling around after the whistle had stopped play, and Chip could see that they had a running argument going. The referee had tried to put a stop to it by calling a roughness penalty on the center, but neither had backed down much.

With two minutes left, Willow Creek drove their way to the 16-yard line. There they faced a third down with three yards to go for a first. Both teams' reserves were on their feet, crowding around their coaches at the end of the field where the action had moved. *This is just like the volleyball game,* Chip thought, watching Coach Ray pace a tight circle. When the coach suddenly wheeled and searched through the ranks of his substitutes, Chip was the only one with half an eye on him. Coach had that look that said he was sending someone into the game. He looked straight into Chip's eyes. Chip started forward, pointing to himself with a questioning look. But the coach's eyes darted away and he grabbed another boy near him. "Go in for Rogers. Tell Baxter to switch over to the right side. That's where they've been makin' all their yards. We've got to stop that play!"

Well, he's just going in for one play, shrugged Chip. *It's no big deal to be a messenger boy.* The coach's move had been a good one though, he thought. By the time Willow Creek noticed the change, it would be too late for them to change the play.

Chip saw the red and blue units grimly take their positions. Even with the dirt and grass stains, their colors still sparkled under the lights. The red backfield charged to their left, as Chip had seen them do countless times that game, with the runner following two blocking backs behind his left tackle. They hadn't expected Baxter to shift! The huge Forest Grove lineman plowed into the blockers like a tractor pulling a heavy load. Slowly, he forced his man right into the path of the runner. Then his long arms grabbed the runner around the waist.

"We got 'em! We got 'em!" shouted Coach Ray, jabbing a fist in the air. All the Forest Grove players began to whoop but were brought short by Bronc's booming voice. "Reverse!" he yelled. Confused, Chip squinted through the scattered piles of players, and then he saw it. Somehow, the running back had sneaked the ball to a wide receiver going in the opposite direction. The player Roosevelt had just stopped did *not* have the ball. All the Forest Grove players had been drawn in to stop Willow Creek's favorite play. Only Rennie and Bruce recovered quickly enough to have a chance to stop the runner racing around right end. Bruce was ambushed by a block from the quarterback, which slowed him up long enough to keep him a step behind the runner.

"Rennie, get him!" shrieked Coach Ray. Chip was thankful that the earlier hard tackle hadn't slowed Rennie. With long, quick strides, Rennie closed in on the runner near the far sideline. But Willow Creek apparently had their fastest runner carrying the ball. He sped toward the goal line, inches from his cheering teammates bunched along the sideline.

Since the action was clear across the field, it was hard for Chip to see exactly what was happening. At first, Rennie seemed to have a chance at him, then the runner seemed to be sprinting into the clear. Too late to get a good shot at him, Rennie stretched out one arm to grab the Willow Creek runner's elbow as he went by near the 5-yard line. The runner pulled away, but suddenly whirled and dove toward Rennie, who was sprawled near the sideline. The ball had popped out and was tumbling just out of Rennie's reach near the chalk line.

Hundreds of voices seemed to be shouting, "Fumble!" Bronc still managed to be heard, bellowing, "Get it before it rolls out-of-bounds!" As the Willow Creek boy scrambled over Rennie to reach the ball, Bruce dove in and knocked him away. Chip couldn't tell if Bruce was out-of-bounds or not when he covered the ball. The Willow Creek coach signaled vigorously that he was. If true, the ball would go back to Willow Creek. But an official peered down briefly, then swung his arm in a wide arc toward the Willow Creek goal.

"Our ball! Our ball!" yelled Coach Ray.

Chip found himself joining Dan and P.C. as they gave each other a joyful victory pounding. "Did you see him run? That Rennie can sure scoot!" marveled P.C. as he jumped on Dan's back.

"He saved the game!" said Dan, flipping him into Chip's waiting arms. "We won it. They can't get the ball back! With only a minute to go, Scot can just fall on the ball until time runs out."

The Forest Grove players on the field ran over to congratulate Rennie and Bruce. Their departure left two boys in the middle of the field, one of them being held back by the referee. The other, the Willow Creek center, hovered menacingly nearby.

"Uh-oh," said Dan. "If that's who I think it is, we could be in trouble."

The referee pushed the boy back with a stern warning. It was blue uniform 55. "So Eric's fighting with that center," laughed Chip. "Big deal! I hope they knock each other silly!"

Dan grabbed Chip's elbow and pointed to a bright yellow object wadded on the ground near the line of scrimmage. "Maybe it's a bigger deal than you think. There's a penalty on the play. If it's on Eric, it could give them the ball back. And I have a sneaking suspicion from the way that center is clapping his hands that it *is* on Eric!"

73

The Forest Grove players who had mobbed Rennie and Bruce now crowded around the two officials. The group shrank back only after the referee ordered them away. He held out his hands and his partner flipped the ball to him. The stunned Forest Grove players parted grudgingly as he marched through them toward the Forest Grove goal. Setting the ball gently on the 8-yard line, he signaled a first down for Willow Creek. Then he stepped back and made a motion to both benches.

"Personal foul, face mask!" groaned Coach Ray. Chip had never seen the coach's face so red. In fact, he hadn't ever seen a human being that color. Chip expected the man to blow up at any time. But he just stomped his foot and turned his back on the field, covering his eyes with one hand.

"Craig! What have you got out there?" Bronc shouted to the referee.

The man jogged slowly over, leaving behind him a trail of dejected Forest Grove starters. "I've got number 55 on the blue team with a personal foul," he sighed. "He grabbed the boy by the face mask and pulled pretty hard. I know it's a tough break, but that's one I've got to call!"

Bronc rubbed a hand over his bald spot while he ground his gum. "How about the other kid? Didn't he do anything to start it?"

"Oh, they've both been looking for trouble. To tell you the truth, I probably should have thrown them both out of the game long ago. But no, I didn't see the center do anything illegal on *this* play. It's a first down for the red."

The lineup for the Forest Grove defense hadn't changed. But it was hard to believe that they were the same group that had fought off Willow Creek just a minute ago. The pent-up energy that had been building all evening had finally been let loose in a premature celebration. Now the blue-shirted team looked tired,

74

confused, and beaten as they lined up. It took only two plays for Willow Creek to run the ball in for the winning score.

It was like watching a movie that ended tragically in the middle of a funny scene. Chip couldn't believe it was over. Like most of his teammates, he stared at the leaps, hugs, and whoops being performed on the far side of the field. He kept waiting for someone to change the referee's decision, or to give them another chance, or something. But nothing could be done.

Coach Ray sent them on their way, muttering only about "bad breaks" and "nice tries." Chip had begged a ride home with Dan and his parents, but he risked lingering a few seconds near the coach. He suspected that Eric might not have heard the last of what had gone on. Sure enough, Coach Ray caught Eric by the arm and pulled him back, quietly but firmly. Chip shuffled away slowly with his head on his chest, as if depressed about the game. Listening carefully, he heard, "I told you back in practice that we don't play that way on this team. No, I don't want to hear any excuses. I know what kind of kid you were up against, and I know it wasn't easy. But you have to keep your head in this game. Your temper cost us the game. A lot of fine effort just went down the drain. It's fine with me if we get beat by a better team, but I am not going to stand around and watch us beat ourselves. You're back on the bench until . . ."

Chip had heard enough. As he broke into a run, the close loss was the last thing on his mind. There was a linebacker position open. And now he had a fighting chance to earn it before his dad came to watch him.

In practice that week, Chip learned a lesson about the power of fear: one big fear can wipe out a lot of little ones. Chip was so desperate to have his dad see him start that he pushed all caution aside. Whenever there

75

was a runner or blocker in sight, Chip ran in to challenge him, without any debate. He struggled away from blockers as if fighting for his very life. On one play, he ran right over Rennie's block, ignored Bruce's fake, and latched onto the fullback's leg. There he hung like a leech until more teammates arrived.

"If he's such a bad player, why can't you block him?" Bruce scolded Rennie.

The play drew no comment from the coaches, but Chip knew that they were watching him. He was going to make them notice him if he had to make every tackle this afternoon. On the next play, though, he found out that it wasn't going to be so easy. He had caught Rennie off his guard. The starters had been going at three-quarters speed, as they often did in practice. But Chip had woken them up. Embarrassed they started to put out a better effort.

Chip fought harder than ever, though, as the afternoon wore on. He even embarrassed himself with his loud grunt as he fought in vain to force his way through a wall of blockers on a pass rush. But nobody else seemed to notice. As Chip looked around, he saw Eric quietly return to his position. *He hasn't said a word all afternoon,* Chip noted with a smile. Eric hadn't been in on many tackles, either. He spent most of the time looking at the ground, avoiding eye contact with anyone. Like an athlete who discovers his opponent is weakening, Chip felt even stronger as he watched Eric struggle.

It was at the following practice that Dan called together the "Left Side Three," as P.C. had named them. "How are we doing in our contest?" he asked.

"Still sixty-four yards behind going into today," answered P.C. Chip could not imagine how P.C. kept the running count in his head. After all, the guy wasn't that good a student.

Dan leaned in closer to the two and whispered, "I've

76

been keeping my eyes open and I've finally found the offense's fatal weakness. Believe me this is going to help us beat the right side. You'll never guess what the weak spot is!"

After a short pause, P.C. said, "Well, if we can't guess what it is, what's the point of making us guess? What's their weak spot?"

Dan looked each boy straight in the eye. "Roosevelt."

P.C. hung his arm around Dan's neck. "Medic!" he called. "I think this boy's been knocked dingy. We'll find a nice, padded cell for you."

"Shhh!" whispered Dan. "You'll give away the secret. I'm serious. I've been studying him for a long time, and I found a tip-off. When Roosevelt gets set to block for a run, he puts all his weight forward. That makes his knuckles turn white. When he's blocking for a pass, he sits back on his heels because he doesn't have to charge forward. I can tell you every time if it's a pass or run just by the color of his knuckles."

"Sure," said P.C. "What's your signal going to be?"

"Let's keep it simple. I'll just brush my leg if it's a pass; otherwise, it's a run."

"This I've got to see," said Chip, backpedaling to his position. No sooner had the offense lined up than Dan started rubbing his leg. Chip looked at P.C., who shrugged and backed up a few steps. Both players were so amazed that the tip turned out to be true that they merely gawked as Gary Rogers caught a pass between them.

"Didn't you see my signal?" asked Dan.

"Sorry. I'll believe you now," said P.C.

This is perfect! thought Chip, watching Dan move back into his lineman's stance. *Dan's tip-off can't help but make me look good.*

Dan left his leg alone on the next play, and quickly both P.C. and Chip crept closer to the line of scrimmage. Both bolted into the backfield the instant the ball was snapped, and they tackled Rennie before he had taken two steps.

"They were offside," complained Scot. "They had to be!" But neither of the coaches backed up his argument; instead they chewed out the blockers on the right side. By the time Coach Ray whistled the starters off and let the offensive reserves run some plays, the Left Side Three had narrowed the gap in their contest to seventeen yards.

Chip, P.C., and Dan manhandled the reserves with greater ease than they had the starters, even without Roosevelt in the lineup to accidentally tip off the plays. After each tackle, Chip looked up at the coaches for some word of approval. Coach Ray ignored him, concentrating on what the blockers were doing wrong. Chip hadn't expected the older coach to say much, but he couldn't figure out why Bronc was so silent. *He must still be thinking of that punt,* he thought. *He knows I had a good practice before that game, and then bombed in the game. But what more can a guy do in one practice?*

Again, it was Dan who came to the rescue. "Say, this is my lucky day! I wonder if the CIA has any openings," he grinned. "Chip, take a good look at Gary before he goes out for a pass."

"Forget it," said Chip. "He's P.C.'s man on passes. I'm supposed to watch the backs."

"That kind of thinking never got anyone into the Hall of Fame," said Dan. "Whenever he's the main pass target, he suddenly starts acting really cool and relaxed. It's a poor acting job covering up the fact that the play is going to him."

"So Gary won't win any Oscars," said Chip. "What's that have to do with me?"

"Oh, I was just thinking that you could trail him and cut in front to intercept. But if that's too much bother . . ."

78

For a while, Chip wished Dan had kept this advice to himself. Every time he thought he saw Gary make a suspicious move, he followed him. As a result, he was caught out of position on a couple of plays. *That isn't going to impress the coach,* Chip thought angrily. After that, he ignored Dan's latest hint and was in on several more tackles.

Just when Chip expected the long practice to be called off, Coach Ray ordered the first team back in. Chip's legs ached and his muscles were starting to feel slow and numb. Only the sight of Eric tripping on his own cleats from tiredness spurred him back to his high level of effort.

Then he saw it! Dan hadn't exaggerated when he said Gary was a poor actor. Chip had been looking for subtle changes in Gary's stance and walk. But there was no mistaking the difference this time. Gary looked sleepily at Chip and P.C., and even yawned while the quarterback barked out signals. He was the last to bend down and take his stance, as if he didn't care whether the play worked or not. Out of the corner of his eye, Chip saw Dan brush his leg. It was a pass play all right!

I hope Dan knows what he's doing, thought Chip. He inched to the outside, as warily as an inmate sneaking out of a jail. Scot shouted "Hut-three," and Gary lazily jogged toward the middle of the field. Keeping his eyes on the quarterback, Chip shadowed the receiver, staying a good five yards away from him. For a split second, he checked to see where Rennie was. The speedy back had stopped blocking for Scot and started downfield.

That's my man! Chip thought. A wave of fear swept over him. If Dan was wrong and the pass was to Rennie, Chip would look like a total fool. Suddenly, Gary burst into a sprint, and cut sharply to his right. Chip and P.C. both scrambled after him, P.C. in the rear, Chip moving between Gary and the quarterback.

Chip saw Scot release the ball. He had only to move two more steps before the ball hit him near the throat. Without even juggling it, Chip snatched the ball and raced downfield.

After crossing the practice field goal line, Chip flipped the ball high in the air, caught it, and trotted back toward the coaches. Coach Ray had seen enough from his offense. He ordered the team off the field, and unleashed a parting shot at Scot. "What kind of pass was that?"

Bronc took the ball from Chip and winked at him. "That was a professional move you made there," he said, rubbing his sleeve over his bald spot. "You took a big gamble, you know. But that's what great plays are made of."

"I just guessed right on the play," Chip beamed. He was enjoying Bronc's puzzled look. It looked as if the assistant coach were trying to figure out which Chip was the real one, the timid bumbler or the bold gambler.

Bruce whistled. "Don't suppose you could pull off one of those interceptions in a real game, do you?"

"Yeah, I couldn't believe it," marveled Rennie. "The pass was right in his hand, and he didn't drop it."

Flushed with success, Chip could afford to toss off Rennie's comment with a laugh. Nearly everyone on the team came up to him to offer some comment on the interception. And even Rennie said, right out loud, that he thought Coach Ray would have to start him on Tuesday.

"You put us fifty-three yards in the lead," called P.C. as he turned to ride his bike down the hill.

Waving proudly to P.C., Chip finally noticed Dan fumbling at the combination to his bike lock. "You were right about Gary," Chip laughed. "He really is a bad actor."

"Right," said Dan quietly.

80

7
The Mud Bowl

When the rains finally arrived, they tried to make up for their month's tardiness in a single, week-long cloudburst. The torrent fell so hard all weekend that even a quick dash from a car door to a house couldn't be done without a drenching. Football practice had to be canceled on Monday, and even by game time on Tuesday a light drizzle was still falling.

Mr. Demory leaned out of the front seat of his car and snapped open his umbrella. Picking his way through the puddles in the parking lot, he arrived at the other door just as his wife got out. Jill, standing safely on a high spot on the asphalt, looked over the field from under her rain parka. "Look at that mess!" she laughed. "Is that where you're going to play?"

The Brycelin Heights field had suffered the same fate as the Forest Grove practice field. The dryness had withered the grass, most of which had been worn away.

Now the rain had softened the hard dirt, leaving a muddy swamp with sparse patches of green poking through it. The midfield was dotted with small ponds of standing water. Although the field's boundaries were chalked, the lines were spotty, since there was little solid material for the chalk to hold on to.

"Oh, Chuck, they're not going to play in that!" said Mrs. Demory.

"Football is a game played under any and all weather conditions," started Mr. Demory. But as he noticed the ripples in the standing water, he, too, frowned.

Chip was the last out of the car. After lacing his shoes, he took a deep breath and stretched his arms, as he had seen Jill do before her game. "A little water never hurt anyone," he said. His only worry was that the coaches might be tempted to call off the contest.

"Where is Tom tonight?" said Mom. "I thought he mentioned something about coming along."

"You know, I haven't had time to get back to him," said Chip. "I've just been so busy this week." He really hadn't been that busy, but he didn't see why Tom should have to come with. He waved and went off to look for the coaches. It was close to game time, and no one had yet announced who was starting in place of Eric.

Apparently, Coach Ray had doubts about the field, too. Chip found him by the end zone with the Brycelin Heights coach, pointing at the field. After a lot of headshaking and shrugging, the two parted.

Chip heard the snap of gum just before the hand touched his shoulder. "You're starting at left linebacker," said Bronc. Chip turned and broke into a grin. He wished he had a tape recorder so he could play those words over again and again. "You're starting at left linebacker," he repeated to himself.

Bronc seemed unaware of the emotions bubbling in the boy. "We felt you earned the shot in practice," he went on in his grave, pregame voice. "You've been with us long enough to know what you're doing out there. Let's see a good effort. Be a tiger out there, remember!"

Chip nodded. Bronc could have asked him to stand on his head in the mud and he would have done it. "I'm a starter!" he said out loud to himself. He searched for his family and found them in the middle of a group of parents, most of whom huddled miserably in the drizzle. Chip wanted to rush over and tell them the news, but then he remembered it would not be news to them. For all they knew, he had always been a starter. *Well, just wait until they see me run out on the field,* he thought.

Brycelin Heights started the game dressed completely in white with purple numbers and helmets. But already their legs were plastered with muddy spots. They seemed to have only half the number of players as Forest Grove, and Chip had the feeling that meant they weren't that good a team. His hunch seemed to be right as Forest Grove drove down the field the first time they got the ball. Rennie was slipping all over like a deer on ice, and so the team went to their strongest ball carrier, Bruce. There was nothing fancy about the attack. Just Bruce running between the tackles, and ramming forward for about five yards a try.

Chip, meanwhile, hopped up and down on the sidelines. He was trying to stay loose, and at the same time get rid of extra energy. While the offense drove down the field, he pictured himself making tackles and interceptions. Already covered from the top of his helmet to his toes in mud, Bruce ended the long march by sliding into the end zone.

Here we go! thought Chip. But to his disgust, Brycelin Heights fumbled the kickoff. The ball kept squirting out of piles of players like a greased eel until Roosevelt finally surrounded it at the 23-yard line. That meant more minutes of waiting while the offense

went at it again. The Brycelin Heights defense stiff-
ened, but Forest Grove was finally able to score on a
fourth-down run by Scot. The first quarter had almost
ended, and Chip hadn't gotten into the game yet.

"Come on, hang on to it this time," he muttered as
Scot prepared to kick off.

"Whose side are you on, anyway?" asked Dan.

"All right, defense! Let's go!" shouted Coach Ray, as
Brycelin Heights took over the ball. Chip turned to
make sure his folks were watching. No, they weren't!
They seemed to be having a good chat with the people
next to them. Chip lingered as long as he dared with
his helmet off so they could still spot him if they liked.
Finally Jill waved and nudged her dad, and Chip raced
onto the field. This time was worlds different from the
last time he had entered a game. He *belonged* on the
field; he had earned his spot. He wasn't just filling in
for a few plays as someone's sub. Instinctively, he
stepped away from the middle linebacker. But then he
remember it wasn't Eric. Bruce had moved over from
the outside to fill his spot, while Chip had taken over
for Bruce. Where was Eric, anyway? Chip glanced at
the sidelines but did not see him.

"Let's see you play like you did in practice," said
Bruce.

Chip grinned. He certainly planned to. This taste of
success made him feel stronger and faster than he had
ever felt. As the Brycelin Heights players came to the
line, Chip crouched low, coiled for action. He was
probably the only player on the field who wasn't thinking about the horrid playing conditions. That proved
costly on the first play. The running back darted to his
side of the line, and Chip slid off the block of the right
end. When the back cut to the inside, Chip planted his
foot sharply to cut with him. His foot slid out from
under him. Before he could even get his hands out to
break the fall, he landed heavily on his seat, splashing

mud around him. With Chip out of the way, the runner gained nearly fifteen yards.

Shocked by the coldness as the water penetrated his uniform, and trying to ignore his bruised tailbone, Chip returned to his position. He shook the mud off his fingers and looked for a clean spot on his pants to wipe them off. Chip braced himself for some smart comments by his teammates, but no one said a word. As he had already found out, it wasn't a chatty group on defense. They took their jobs seriously. Judging by the way many of them grimaced as they walked around in the slop, they weren't enjoying the conditions.

It's a wet field, you dummy, Chip scolded himself. *You can't make sharp cuts on a field like this. Pay attention now.* He didn't need to worry for a while. On the next play, the ball carrier suffered a similar embarrassment as he slipped, skated a few steps, and finally fell without a player near him. The next two plays went to the other side of the field, where they were stopped short of the first down. Chip jogged off the field as Brycelin Heights prepared to punt.

Before he reached the sidelines, he again searched out his parents. He longed to run over to them to hear their reactions. Was his dad growling advice that no one would ever hear, as he did when Jill played? But he also felt, as never before, that he was part of the team. He would have to try and forget about Mom and Dad until the game was over.

With Forest Grove safely ahead by two touchdowns, Chip secretly cheered for the Brycelin Heights defense. He had enjoyed being in the game so much he could hardly stand pacing the sidelines. The sooner he could get back on the field, the better. Seconds later, Scot bobbled the snap from center and accidently kicked it forward. When the teams unpiled, the referee had to ask the boy on the bottom which team he was on. The mud-caked lad turned out to be from the home team.

"Defense!" shouted Coach Ray.

The deep breath Chip took as he sprinted out felt so fresh! "This is great!" Chip said to himself. This time the quiet of the field felt strange. No one else seemed to be having such fun. What was the matter with them? Instead, he heard murmurings, some of them pretty foul, about the weather and the field. All the grumbling took some of the excitement away, but Chip played well for the rest of the half. Neither team had chosen to pass with the wet football, and the offenses were bogging down. With the lead still 14-0 at the halftime break, Coach Ray announced that it would be a good chance for the reserves to see some action. Everyone seemed thrilled with that news. In fact, Chip thought the grimy starters cheered more loudly than the reserves.

Chip bit his lip, thinking the fun was over. But then Bronc called him over. "We're leaving you in. You can use the experience."

As Chip looked over the group that charged on the field with him to start the second half, he felt almost cocky. With the other starters all on the bench, that made Chip the best player on the field. He caught himself starting to give out advice to the others until he saw that Eric was now in the game.

"Hey, help me pin this on!" said P.C., who had come in at defensive back. He pulled a stiff sheet of paper from under his jersey and a safety pin from his hip pad. The large letters on the tag spelled "Killer."

Chip gawked at him. "You're crazy!"

"So? Come on!" begged P.C., eyeing the Brycelin Heights huddle. "I've wanted to do this all my life." As Chip made no move to help, P.C. chuckled, "All right, I'll do it myself." As he pinned on his name tag, several teammates broke out in laughter and jostled those next to them to look. Even the Brycelin Heights tackle noticed and started snickering.

What a nut! smiled Chip as P.C. strode around, soaking up the attention. *I'll bet Coach Ray is having a fit.*

If P.C.'s fun was upsetting the coach, at least it didn't last long. On the first play, P.C. helped out on the tackle and found half his tag ripped away when he stood up.

"Hey, what happened, Killer?" teased his teammates.

"Just call me P.C. now," he said sadly. "Killer lies buried somewhere around the 35-yard line."

The wind had shifted direction and was now gusting from the north. It cut through their uniforms, chilling their bones as the temperature seemed to drop by the minute. By this time, the field had been almost totally chewed up. From one 30-yard line to the other, not a blade of grass was left standing in the center of the field.

"Isn't this great?" howled P.C.

Chip felt a little warmer just hearing his cheerful chatter. "You like the mud, huh?" he asked.

"Like it? I love it. This is how football was meant to be played—in the middle of a rice paddy."

P.C.'s enthusiasm was contagious. Although the lineup was full of reserves, the defense swarmed all over the Brycelin Heights team, charging and leaping through the muck like kittens with a new toy. After stopping their opponents on three plays, they ran off the field, dripping wet but laughing, while a new unit took over on offense. Coach Ray, his clipboard tucked under his elbow, looked on curiously. Chip noticed the man was standing straight up, instead of hunched over like a coiled spring, his usual stance during a game. Somehow this contest had lost much of its meaning for the coach. He apparently had no doubt that Forest Grove would win.

Sure enough, the offense scored again to make it

87

21-0. The defense galloped onto the field, purposely sending a shower of mud on each other. This time Chip led the way. It felt as refreshing as the first time he got permission to run outside in the rain with a swimsuit on.

"Yoweee!" howled P.C. as he charged in to help finish off a tackle. "Way to go, you mud puppies!"

The time between plays got to be as much fun as the actual plays as P.C. triggered an unending stream of jokes and teasing. "I give up!" he announced. "I can't tell who's on what team anymore. From now on, I'm tackling anything that moves in my area."

"Better be careful," Chip warned. "We found a few alligators living in this during the first half."

"Speaking of safety," P.C. grinned. "Maybe we should form a buddy system out here in case someone goes in over his head."

"It's too late," said another boy. "I think we lost Peterson on the last play."

"Call a time-out!" said P.C. "Ask the ref if we can form a human chain and find him."

Brycelin Heights was unable to cross midfield the rest of the day. Meanwhile, the Forest Grove offense was content to run time off the clock. The fourth quarter flew by, and Forest Grove finished with an easy 21-0 win. As the defense ran off the field, Chip saw P.C. go into a baseball slide which carried him nearly to the sidelines.

"Look at you!" said Chip's mom as Chip came over to accept their congratulations. "You're filthy!" She shook her head and then added, "It was fun to see you play. But you were all so dirty it was hard for me to see which one was you."

"Nice game, Chip," said Dad. "But you'd better keep your distance until we get you hosed off. Don't ask me how we're going to get you home without ruining the interior of our car."

"You did great!" Jill added, wiping a blotch of mud off his nose. "Say, who's the little guy who played with you in the second half? He's a riot!"

Basking in their compliments, Chip didn't recognize that he was being asked a question. "Well, the coach is calling," he beamed. "I'd better get over and see what he has to say. Be with you in a minute."

Sensing that his players were getting chilled, Coach Ray limited his postgame summary to a brief notice of when the next practice was. As Chip listened, he saw one pair of white pants standing out like a spotlight from the rest of the team. It was Dan. Obviously, everyone had gotten into the game except him. The thought of Dan being left out took some of the silliness out of Chip, and he started to edge through the players towards him. Just then the meeting broke up, and everyone scattered to their cars. Before Chip could get to Dan, he bumped into Bruce.

"Hey, you really played a good game," Chip said.

"Oh, it was pretty easy," Bruce said. The next sentence clued Chip in as to why Bruce was talking so softly. "Hey, there's going to be a party at Scot's house on Friday. It's for starters only, and I guess you qualify now."

"Just got in under the wire," said Chip.

"Yeah, well, it's a good break all around. None of us were too thrilled about having to let Eric in. He's really bad news. But now he's out and you're in, so no sweat. Don't go telling anyone about it, though. It's only for starters."

Chip saw the white pants as they moved slowly across the parking lot. "But what about the Atkinsons? Dave's a starter, but Dan isn't. Being they're twins, he's going to know, isn't he?"

"Naw, Dave can keep quiet about it. By the way, there'll be some girls there."

"Really?" said Chip. "Like who?"

Bruce grinned secretively. "Nothin' but the best. Tammy, Gail, Laura, and a few of their friends. Now don't go telling anyone," he repeated as he walked off.

Dan had already disappeared by then, and Chip trudged off to his family. His muscles were starting to ache from fatigue. But it was a pleasant ache that kept reminding him of all he had done that night. Shivering slightly, he found his way back to the parking lot, where his dad had already warmed up the car. He didn't even mind when his dad asked him to take off his jersey and put it in the trunk. Scrunching in the warm backseat, sitting on sections of shopping bags that Jill had ripped up, he enjoyed answering Jill's questions about football. Occasionally, she had to repeat herself because Chip's thoughts kept wandering to the game and to the party on Friday. *I can't believe it! I've actually done it!* he thought.

8
Injury

There was no reason why Bruce should have made such a big deal out of hushing up the party. By the time Chip reached school on Monday, everyone on the team knew about it. Scot, Rennie, and some of the others were even talking about it right in front of the rest.

Chip and P.C. paired up for the prepractice calisthenics. One would hold the other's leg or legs while he did sit-ups or stretches, and then they would switch off. Chip was reaching out to touch his toes when P.C. first brought it up. "Pretty wild party from what I hear. Were you there?"

"Yeah, I was there, but you heard wrong," Chip said. He finished his last two sit-ups and looked at his partner. "Scot's parents were there the whole time, so how wild could it have been?" He had heard some gripes from other reserves about the starters' "private" party, but apparently P.C. held no grudges.

"I should ask my folks if we can have a scrub party at my house," he said as he let go of Chip's ankles. "Of course, we'd have to call it something else," he frowned. "I mean, if you call it a scrub party, everyone would think all we're going to do is wash floors or something. Nah, it probably wouldn't be much. What kind of girls could you get to come to a scrub party?"

Your party would probably be a lot more fun, Chip thought, grabbing P.C.'s ankles. With his partner silenced for a moment by the strain of the exercise, Chip thought back on the evening. He had been so tickled to go he could hardly believe it was true. Some of the most popular girls were there, ones he'd never even talked to. Just by being at the party he had shown that he was important, a starter on the football team. He had been so flushed with the honor that, for a while, he had convinced himself that he was having a good time. But he had begun to feel more and more awkward. *Just what's going on?* he had finally asked himself. He was sitting in a stuffed chair in the corner, trying to act like an adult like everyone else. Sure, the girls were cute, but they didn't seem anything like Jill. They were just trying to seem important, like he was. After a while he had gotten tired of running down the reserves and laughing at some of the dumb plays they had made. *They could really have a great time talking about all the dumb things I've done since I came out,* he realized. Then Bruce had finally gotten a card game going, and Chip had spent the rest of the evening at the table either watching or playing.

Now P.C. could really give a party! Chip thought to himself as Coach Ray whistled a stop to the exercises. The coach continued to use the starters on offense in practice scrimmages, leaving Chip with his old "Left Side Three" gang. Unfortunately, the third member of the group didn't have much to say. Dan was still upset about being the only one on the team who didn't get in

92

the last game. Chip tried to ask him about it once, and Dan mumbled, "It was a mistake. The coaches told me they were sorry and said they had too much to think about to keep track of everything. Coach Ray said they ought to have a student manager or something to handle the little things so they wouldn't get distracted."

Chip couldn't think of anything helpful to say, and Dan wearily took up his position in front of Roosevelt. He wasn't giving out any tip-offs from Roosevelt, and he gave more ground than usual to the blocker in front of him. Chip shook his head. *Must be rough having to face Roosevelt every single practice.* P.C. continued to banter, even though Dan wasn't responding. But then P.C. could keep up a running conversation with the grass.

It was the first cold day of the fall. Chip tucked his hands inside his sleeves while waiting for the first play. Quickly, though, he poked them back out when he saw Eric purposely roll his sleeves up to the elbow. Chip had a feeling that the middle linebacker was starting to resurface after a peaceful week and a half. Ever since his crucial penalty against Willow Creek, Eric had tried to melt into the background. He had said almost nothing. When he played, it was listlessly, as if he could best avoid attention if he stayed away from tackling the ballcarrier.

No one had been too hard on him about blowing that game, at least not to his face. But there had been enough comments behind his back, especially among the starters, who hated to think of their unbeaten record being ruined by that call. Eric must have overheard a few of those, and he probably imagined the rest. It was obvious after the first play of practice that he was starting to fight back. On a simple running play, Eric threw one blocker to the ground and blasted Bruce with all his might. Bruce gasped and brought his feet up to his chest, the wind knocked out of him.

93

"What do you think you're doing?" spat Scot. "That was a cheap shot!"

Chip saw the starters gather around Bruce and glare at Eric. Bruce had already recovered and was slowly getting up. Chip thought he heard him muttering swear words at Eric. Lashing out at the whole lot, Eric sneered, "What's the matter? Can't take a little hit?" With that, Eric's mouth got going. He shot a cutting remark at someone after nearly every play. Chip realized that the peaceful era of playing next to Eric was over. Sooner or later, he knew, Eric would start in on him again.

Chip's turn did not come until midway through practice. Several plays had driven home the fact to Chip that he wasn't a star because of natural talent. He had won his starting job with a determined, almost desperate energy, far beyond the practice level of most boys. But when he routinely chased Rennie on a quick pass to the right halfback, Rennie faked him completely off his feet. As he sprawled on the ground, he heard that familiar voice. "Nice tackle, all-star!"

Their truce dissolved. Chip found himself more angry than ever at his enemy. This time he could fight back, because *he* was the starter. "Like to see you do better, scrub!" A flash of hatred in Eric's eyes showed that Chip had found the perfect weapon against Eric's mocking title. Eric stopped calling him "all-star," although Chip continued to throw in a few more "scrub" remarks at him, just for good measure.

The victory didn't last long. Chip realized that it was Eric who was now playing with a desperate, almost enraged force. When Eric—who was stronger and a little more coordinated than Chip—played that way, Chip began to worry about his starting job.

"Hey, Dan! What about those tip-offs about whether it's a run or a pass?" Chip pleaded. Dan squinted at him as if he didn't know what he was talking about, then nodded slowly.

"Yeah, we've fallen behind the right side again. They've got two yards on us," added P.C.

Seeing no signal from Dan on the next play, Chip wondered if his tall friend was back at his detective work or not. He decided to gamble that no signal meant a run was coming, and moved up next to Dan. Sure enough, it was a quick burst off tackle. Although Roosevelt pushed Dan out of the way, Chip filled the gap with only one blocker between him and the ball-carrier. Rennie ordinarily considered blocking a neces-sary evil, and Chip had found it easy to fend him off. But on this occasion, Rennie flung himself at just the right spot to knock Chip to his knees. Bruce ran past him before being brought down by the pursuing Eric. As the middle linebacker stomped back to his position, he said, "We'll see who's the scrub!"

Chip glanced nervously at the coaches. They were huddled together, looking at Eric. It hadn't been his play that had benched him before; it was his temper. Chip noted, sadly, that Eric had walked away from several players who had wanted to goad him into a fight after his hard tackle of Bruce. *How am I going to keep my job?* he thought. *I did pretty well against Brycelin Heights, but is that going to be enough?* Spurred on again by Dan's signals, Chip fought hard to outshine his rival.

On one play to the other side of the field, Chip sprinted all the way to his right, hoping to cut off the run. "Reverse!" came P.C.'s voice from back across the field. Chip froze and saw that the offense was trying a trick reverse just like the one Willow Creek had used. But he knew before he even turned that he was trapped way out of position. Eric had spotted the deception before Chip, but even he wasn't going to reach the ballcarrier. Scot blocked out P.C., and the play went for a touchdown.

"Duh, I'm Chip Demory!" Eric started hollering in

95

a dopey voice. "I don't have more'n a little bitty part of a brain. You can fake me out of my shoes, my socks, my underwear, you name it. Yessir, try anything on me, I'll fall for it."

"Shut up, scrub!" Chip shot back, but the name had lost its force. They both knew that if Chip kept making mistakes and Eric kept up his good play, there would be a new starter come Wednesday night against Van Buren. Chip looked around at his defensive mates and found some laughing. *So I make mistakes,* Chip thought. *I'm still new at this, you creeps.*

"Keep it up, all-star," laughed Eric.

As he had many times before, Chip searched his mind for some chance to get even. But this time he found something to work with. Chip picked up the clue when it dawned on him that the offense wasn't gloating over the play. On the very next play, Chip charged past a weak block by Gary, the end, and stopped Rennie in the backfield.

"Nice play," said Bruce loudly.

It seemed almost too easy. On the next play, Gary completely missed his block on Chip. Rennie, blocking for Bruce, ignored Chip and headed out to block P.C. That left Chip with a clear shot at Bruce and he stopped him for a loss.

"Can't anyone block this guy?" Bruce said as he slammed the ball down. But he winked at Chip as he turned. Then Chip saw another wink from Gary. As Coach Ray stormed over to Gary to show him how to get his body into a block, Chip figured it out. The starters couldn't stand Eric. Bruce had told him that after the last game. That meant they were on his side! They wanted him to keep his job. Those poor blocks had been little gifts to keep him in the running. But with Coach Ray on Gary's back, Chip could expect no more such plays.

That was fine with Chip. Just remembering that he

96

had allies put some of the fight back in him. And while he improved his play, the idea of revenge kept coming back. It was he, Chip, who had the advantage. The one thing Eric wanted, according to Dan, was acceptance from the starters. Thanks to Eric's mouth, that wouldn't happen.

When Coach Ray gave them a five-minute break, Chip decided to put his plan into action. He didn't want to make it obvious, so he stared at Bruce, hoping to attract his attention. When the running back finally did look his way, Chip called him over with a nod of his head. Bruce walked over, spitting his mouthpiece into his hand.

"Are you getting as tired of that blabbermouth as I am?" Chip asked.

Bruce's eyes narrowed as he focused on Eric. "Probably."

"Do you think Roosevelt feels the same way?"

"Why, what have you got in mind?"

Chip grinned. "How about a triple-team block? Next time you're blocking up the middle. Dan is kind of out of it today. Roosevelt could let him go for a play and cream Eric."

"While I get him from the other side," nodded Bruce. "A sandwich."

Chip's eyes lit up. "Now you're talking!"

"My pleasure," said Bruce, and he jogged back to his huddle.

He's been asking for this for a long, long time, Chip smiled to himself as he moved back to the defense. He had sworn he would get revenge. If Eric had kept quiet, he would have forgiven all he had done. But there was no turning back this time. *He won't know what hit him!*

Meanwhile, P.C. had finally gotten Eric to settle down. "Hey, you're ruining my reputation as a motor-mouth," he said to Eric. "Give me a break and leave the jabbering to me. It's the only thing I do well on this field."

Eric had flashed a smile, almost a genuine one. Chip marveled again at the way P.C. could say anything to anyone without getting them mad. On the next two plays, there wasn't one sarcastic remark from the middle linebacker.

Chip knew when he saw the offensive formation that this next one was the play. Dan was indicating a run. Chip saw Bruce fix Eric with a cold glare. It was all Chip could do to keep from standing back and watching. Just before the hike, he backed up so that at least the whole thing would be going on in front of him.

"Hut-one!" Roosevelt brushed past Dan, who stood straight up in surprise. Bruce led the way through the "1" hole and veered toward the right linebacker. Suddenly, he cut back toward the middle. Eric, busy fighting off the center's block, never saw him. Roosevelt blasted Eric from one side just as Bruce hit him from the other. Chip had to admit Bruce was a good actor. He immediately turned upfield and threw a block at the safety. Satisfied that justice had been done, Chip moved over to help on the tackle.

Eric raised himself to one knee but kept both palms on the grass to keep himself from tipping over. When he didn't move, Bronc came over and stared into his eyes. "Why don't you go on the sidelines and walk around for a little bit."

After one wobbly step, Eric steadied himself. By the time he reached the sidelines he was already shaking off that glassy look. He wasn't really hurt, just stunned. Chip smiled to himself as a replacement came in for Eric. *That'll slow him down for a while,* he thought.

It was amazing how much freer Chip felt when Eric wasn't around. For the next ten minutes he felt lighter and faster, as if he had shed a weight from his ankles. His mind seemed to work more clearly, too. On another end sweep to the other side, Chip trailed the play and then checked to make sure the left end wasn't coming around to take a reverse handoff. Without breaking stride, he kept going, and joined a group of defenders who were closing in on Rennie. The running back had waited far too long for his blockers to do their jobs. He was trying to dance away from the tacklers, but too many had arrived. Rennie finally just lowered his head and leaned into the blue-shirted mob. Chip fell beneath him and smelled the musty odor of grass as his head was pushed right down to the grass.

It was then that he heard the cry.

"No! Ow! Ow!"

"Get off him, quick!" ordered Scot.

By the time Chip got to his feet, Coach Ray had pushed back the players. They stood in a tight ring around one boy, who was slamming his fist against the ground. At first Chip thought it was Dan. But then he saw him standing, leaning as close as he could to the injured player. *It must be Dave, then,* Chip thought.

"Ow! Help, please!" Chip saw Dave's leg twisted at a bad angle near the ankle. Coach Ray stared at the leg for a minute, licking his lips. There seemed to be fear in his face as he yelled hoarsely for Bronc. The big assistant forced his way through the pack, and snapped at everyone to move back.

"Don't try to move. Just lie down," he said, easing Dave's helmet off and gently laying his head on the grass. Dave's jaw clenched, but he didn't say another word. Bronc fumbled for keys in his back pocket. Without taking his eyes off Dave, he tossed the keys to Chip and said, "In the gym there's a door by the stairs next to the stage. Get the stretcher and some blankets."

He didn't say to hurry, but Chip dashed off in a panic. Racing through the dark, narrow halls, he came to the gym and found it locked. There were eight keys on Bronc's chain. Chip jammed each of them into the lock and broke out in a sweat as none of them worked. On the second try, one finally slid in. He twisted and pulled until the door finally came open.

By the time he got back, many of the boys had started to leave. Practice had been called off. Bronc flung the blankets on Dave. Working so carefully he seemed to be in slow motion, he maneuvered him onto the stretcher. Coach Ray had backed his van onto the field, and Bronc and Dan lifted Dave into the back. Then Dan climbed in with his brother, and Coach Ray drove off.

Chip started to walk home by himself, feeling a little sick to his stomach. He had heard of football injuries, and even knew a boy whose parents wouldn't let him come out for the sport because they thought it too dangerous. But this was the first time he had actually seen a bad injury. It wasn't anyone's fault. Dave's leg happened to be in the wrong spot when a pile of players fell down. That didn't help to erase the memory of Dave's face, though.

Buttoning his jacket against the cold breeze, he heard a jingling in his pocket. Expecting to find some change, his fingers instead found an unfamiliar, cold object. Chip pulled it out and groaned. Bronc's keys. He had forgotten to return them. From where he stood he could see the truck still in the parking lot. *Of course,* thought Chip. *I've got the keys to his truck, too. Typical dumb move, Demory.*

Bronc was standing next to the truck when Chip arrived, out of breath. He didn't seem surprised or angry. Tucking away his handkerchief and accepting the keys, he said, "There's a mean snap to that wind. Want a ride?"

Chip accepted and climbed into the front seat. Bronc saw him step carefully over a gym bag. "Aw, don't worry about that. Just sweaty clothes that need

100

washing," he said as he started up the truck.

"Sorry about the keys," Chip repeated. "It just slipped my mind. I guess I was kind of shook up."

"I think we all are," said Bronc, popping two sticks of gum into his mouth. Shaking his head, he said, "You know, when I was in college we used to all sit around and say a prayer before the game, asking that no one would get hurt."

"Not a bad idea," Chip said. Something about the way Bronc angrily cranked the wheel made him un-comfortable. He was glad it was only a short drive home.

"You know what the crazy thing was?" Bronc went on. "Some of the same people in on the prayer would lose their heads in the game and start gettin' mad. You can't play that way," he sighed. "You have to take it more seriously. Once you get out of control, it's not a game anymore." He looked at Chip, who wished he could scrunch down and hide from those eyes. "You know, we could have had two bad injuries today."

"What?" said Chip, his voice cracking.

"I've got good eyes and better hearing," said Bronc. "When you don't have any hair, the sound waves get a clear shot to the ears. It looked to me like someone planned to *get* someone."

"What do you mean?" started Chip. But Bronc didn't answer. He pulled up to Chip's house and put the car in park. All Chip heard was the whir of the engine. He knew it was time to drop the charade.

"He had it coming," he said, avoiding Bronc's eyes.

"Revenge and football are a bad mix. He could have been seriously hurt."

Chip felt like pulling open the door, but he knew he couldn't leave yet. Searching for some answer that would satisfy Bronc, he said, "You don't know how much I've taken from that guy. I had to stop it some-how."

"I know what you've put up with," smiled Bronc, pointing to his ears. "Remember how well these work? I wish you could find a better way to solve the problem, though. I've never seen a kid fight so hard to get accepted as Eric. But he does it all wrong. I don't think he has a friend on the team, does he? So you go and get the best players to gang up on him today. You think that'll help?"

"So what do you want me to do?" protested Chip.

"Hey! I don't mean to keep workin' you over, and I'm not here to tell you how to run your life. It's just my job as a coach to tell you there's no place for that nonsense on the field. As far as Eric goes, I wish you would have talked it out earlier, but it's too late for that. I know you're a good guy, Chip. I thought maybe the team could somehow help a kid who's got problems. Looks like we're blowing it, though."

Chip hopped onto the driveway. "Some people are just too far gone to help," he said. He felt a desperate need to slam the door.

Just before it shut, he heard, "Hey, we're all God's children."

Revenge. He had been waiting for the chance all year, and now that he'd finally gotten it, the taste was all bad. Chip plopped down on his bed and ran his feet up the wall. Mom hated it when he did that with his shoes on, but he didn't care at this moment. *Bronc's the one who's wrong about all this,* he decided. *It's always us good guys who get caught. I take all kinds of garbage from Eric all year. The first time I try to fight back, I get jumped on by that big ape. He never cared a bit when Eric was doing all that stuff to me!* Or did he? The more Chip thought about it, the more he admitted that it wasn't like Bronc not to care. He was the coach who knew all the first names, watched out for the subs, and had a private word now and then for everyone.

So what did Bronc want him to do? He wouldn't say. Was he talking about turning the other cheek? Chip had heard that phrase often enough in church.

Come on, this is football, thought Chip. *They'd think you were a coward and walk all over you.* His thoughts drifted back to that crunching triple-team block on Eric. For a second he savored it against all the mean things Eric had done.

But the word *coward* stuck in his mind. How much courage did it take to watch the strongest guys on offense wipe out someone who didn't even know it was coming? Chip's feet dropped back on the bed as he thought about it. That was his problem with Eric: he was afraid of him. Dad had read something at family devotions about trust in God and about courage. "Whom should I fear?" was what Chip remembered of it.

I don't know why I'm afraid of him, but I am, he thought glumly. *Face it, I'm afraid of everyone. A starter on the football team, and I'm still afraid. Football hasn't done a thing for me.*

The door burst open after a knock. "Didn't you hear the phone?" asked his mom. "I was in the basement and thought for sure you'd get it. I finally got there on the sixth ring. Anyway, it's Tom."

"Great," muttered Chip, rolling out of bed. "More problems."

9
Life at the Top

Chip had been successful at avoiding Tom for the past two weeks, at least in public. Much of it was due to luck. Tom happened to be busy completing a computer project for the science fair, and that had kept him from popping in on football practices. Besides that, Chip had managed to be gone whenever Tom had called, and made excuses for not getting back to him. Just to keep Tom from getting too upset, Chip had gone over to his house one Saturday night to watch tv and play chess, Tom's favorite game.

But this time Tom had caught him. Chip hated having the phone in the kitchen, because Mom was close by. She had been wondering aloud what Tom was up to, and was sure to keep an ear on the conversation. "Hello?"

"Hi, Chip. Hey, I got a great surprise for you. Just found out for sure this afternoon. You know how you

104

were feeling bad about no one you knew being out for football, and how you were kind of lonely? Well, better late than never. Good ol' Tom to the rescue!"

Chip stared dumbly at the wall. "You're *not* going out for football," he said, more a prayer than a question.

"Oh, no!" Tom laughed. "You know I wouldn't be much good. I don't even know what's going on half the time, yet. They'd laugh me off the field. What I was going to say is that I was talking with one of the players. You know Dan, right? He's a nice guy and he's into computers, too. Did you know his brother broke his leg?"

"Of course I know, you dope."

"Chip!" scolded his mom.

Chip turned away from her and stretched the phone cord as far toward the stairway as it would go. "I was there when it happened."

"Oh, that's right. Well, we started talking about football, and I said that I liked to watch the games. Then he asked me if I was interested in being a student manager. He said they could use someone who wasn't playing to help out with some details, equipment, keeping charts, and stuff."

"Yeah, and what did you say?" asked Chip. He was sure of the answer, but hoped for a miracle anyway. He felt a headache coming on.

"Sounded great to me!" Tom said. "I told him I thought I could do a good job at it, so he set me up to talk with Coach Marsh."

"And he gave you the job," said Chip.

"I start tomorrow. How's that for wild?"

That pest! thought Chip, then tried to sound excited for Tom's sake. "That's great—but I hope you didn't do it for me. You know, I *have* made quite a few friends lately."

"Aw, I know that. I just thought it would be fun."

105

Chip grabbed the top tray and slid it along the ledge. As the cafeteria line slowed down, he grabbed the tray with both hands and breathed heavily. This was bad news, and it was Bruce, of all people, who had put him in this spot. Bruce had gotten carried away with Scot's idea of a starters' party and had decided to form a starters' club. He called it the "Blue and White Club." Some of the starters were making a big deal out of it. They met before nearly every practice, and shooed away any nonstarter who wandered too close. After the first two meetings, there were no more intruders, as word must have spread. Chip felt bad sitting there while guys like P.C. and Dan looked on from a distance. Once Bronc drove up while they were still meeting, and Chip broke out in a bad case of the guilts.

Bruce had been elected president of the club at the last meeting. He had wasted no time in pushing through his plans of sitting together at lunch and dressing up. As Chip watched the casserole being scooped onto his plate, he looked down at his game jersey. Clean and ironed, it really did look sharp. The starters had secretly agreed on wearing those the day of the game with Van Buren. Chip had told his mom that the whole team was doing it when he showed up in it at breakfast. Sometimes during the morning that big number 57 had made him pretty proud. It was a clear mark for all to see that he was one of the fourteen in school who were good enough to make the Blue and White Club. But at this moment, he wished he could bury it and put on the plainest shirt he owned.

In a few seconds, he would come face-to-face with the Blue and White decree that they would sit together at lunch. Just the starters and no one else. As he shuffled toward the milk and dessert, he saw the group at the long table next to the window in the back. They were being loud enough so that no one in the cafeteria could miss them. But someone had violated the rule.

106

The solid row of jerseys was broken by a red top, a white one, and a striped one. Girls. Chip could see clearly only the one on the end. It was Tammy, whom he'd met briefly at the party. There was a seat open next to her.

Chip picked up his tray and shot a glance at the left side of the room. There was Dan, already in their usual spot. P.C. wasn't there yet, though. Chip checked the ranks of blue jerseys to see if P.C. had somehow wormed his way in there. With both hands clutching the tray, he was helpless to ward off P.C.'s surprise attack. The little defensive back reached over his back and tucked a napkin under Chip's chin.

"Come on, now, slugger, we can't have you slobbering your food all over your nice clean jersey," laughed P.C. "Hey, Dan's finally come back to us from Depressionville. He can hardly wait for you to get over there so I can reveal the weekly figures on our running battle with the right side. We're getting to the end, you know. Only two weeks left." Before Chip could answer, P.C. stuck half a roll in his mouth and went back to his table.

Now what do I do? Chip thought. He looked back at the empty chair next to Tammy. She had at least talked to him at the party, and seemed the friendliest of the girls. Everyone in the place would be able to see that he was sitting with her. If that didn't impress them, what would? *What choice do I have?* Chip finally shrugged. *The starters all sit together. That's the plan.*

He walked stiffly over to the starters. He was torn between trying to avoid the looks of his friends and enjoying the feeling of importance he felt as he saw others eyeing him.

"Hi," said Tammy with a smile.

"Welcome to the bunch," said Bruce. "Pretty wild napkin."

Chip remembered the napkin as everyone at the

107

table laughed. He felt the blood rushing to his face to announce his embarrassment when he realized they thought it was just a gag. "Don't want crumbs on my nice clean jersey," he said, straightening the paper napkin as if it were a tie.

"Isn't this chicken stuff awful?" Tammy asked him as she gingerly chewed her casserole. Chip nodded agreement, though he didn't really think so. As he ate he thought about how the football season was turning out to be everything he had hoped it would be. Except for one thing: he wasn't a star running back yet. *Give it time,* he thought. *It's only my first year.*

The game with Van Buren erased Chip's final fear. Just before the contest, Coach Ray had announced that Eric would start—taking over for the injured Dave Atkinson at right defensive end. *Thank you, God,* thought Chip, trying to hold back a grin. After all these weeks of hassle and the bitter competition of the past week, Eric was finally out of the picture for good! Chip had the left linebacking job to himself! He celebrated by playing one of his better games in a 34-7 win over Van Buren. The highlight had come for him in the fourth quarter. He had been fending off a block, waiting to see if the ballcarrier broke through the center of the line. No runner came through, but the ball did, and it flopped right at Chip's feet. He had fallen on it and then ran off the field, holding it high in the air to show everyone who had recovered it.

Chip expected the final two weeks of the season to fly by in a blur of excitement as he enjoyed his success. But, proud as he was of his efforts, he felt his victory crumbling away. There were too many incidents like those of the Monday after the game.

Chip, Dan, and P.C. had arrived a few minutes early and had talked the new student manager, Tom, into getting a football for them. It was cool and cloudy, and it felt good to warm up by tossing passes to each other. Others apparently liked the idea, too. As more players arrived, Tom got out more footballs and games of catch sprouted up over the whole field. As Chip jogged out for a pass, Dan waved to him twice. That meant he was going to throw it as far as he could. Chip started sprinting as the ball sailed into the air. At first he thought it was too far over his head, but he kept running. Nearly tripping over a hole in the sod, he reached out and caught the ball as he tumbled to the ground. Dan was as astonished by the catch as Chip was, and ran out to congratulate him. Before Dan reached his goal, though, Chip was distracted by a sharp whistle. "Get on over here," Bruce called to him. "Let the scrubs play by themselves."

Chip gaped at him. This Blue and White stuff was getting out of hand. Dumbly, he flipped the ball back to Dan. He still liked being in with the starters, but this was getting plain mean. "Aw, I'm tired, anyway," he said to Bruce, and walked away to wait by himself for the practice to start.

Throughout the practice, Chip felt as though he had a leg on each of two ice floes that were drifting apart. Bruce and Scot were getting so obnoxious about this starter club that the reserves couldn't stand them anymore. Yet, as one who played only defense, Chip still spent most of practice time with the subs. He was getting worn out trying to get along with both sides.

Dan and P.C. had been understanding of the situation so far, and still kept him as part of their Left Side Three. Dan was back to his detective tricks, and had come up with another discovery. "Keep your eye on Scot when he's calling out signals," he whispered to the other two. "Tell me if you don't think he crouches just an inch or so lower just before the ball is hiked."

Three pairs of eyes focused on the quarterback as he called out, "Hut-one! Hut!" It wasn't much of a dip. In fact, Chip was not positive he saw it until P.C. rushed in, rubbing his hands. "By Jove, I think he's got something there!" he said.

All of Dan's tips had given the left side an overwhelming advantage in their secret contest with the right. Chip chuckled to himself when he saw Coach Ray scratching his head after a tackle by the Left Side Three. Since it was obvious that Dan and P.C. weren't the most coordinated people, Chip was getting most of the credit for the puzzling strength of the left side. But on one play, Dan anticipated the hike so well that he got by Roosevelt before the giant tackle could even move. Scot never saw what hit him as Dan tackled him before he could pitch the ball to Bruce.

Coach Ray rushed in to check on who had made the tackle. Seeing it was Dan, he stared at Roosevelt, then at Dan, then back at Roosevelt. "How in blue blazes did that player get by you so quickly?"

Good for you, Dan, Chip thought. Poor Dan deserved a break after the miserable luck he had had all year. But Chip saw Scot shove Dan off with a growl, and most of the other starters glared at him. Bruce reached up to whisper something to Roosevelt, but the tackle shook his head. Chip had seen that look on Bruce's face once before—when he had agreed to that vicious block on Eric.

This team is crazy! thought Chip. *It's like we're enemies. At least Roosevelt has some sense.*

A few plays later, Scot dropped back to pass. He sent all his backs out on pass routes, and that meant Chip was to cover Rennie. That was one situation Chip always hated. Rennie was so fast that Chip was always afraid of getting beaten on a long pass. Aided by Dan's tip-off on the play, he had backed up far enough to give Rennie plenty of room. Sure enough, Rennie was going for the long bomb. Legs churning in a full sprint, he sped downfield so fast that, even with his long lead, Chip fell behind.

Fortunately, Rennie had outrun Scot's throwing arm. Chip saw Rennie look back and suddenly stop. As the running back did so, he slipped to the ground. Chip then turned upfield just as the ball fluttered down. He had only a split second to react. He stuck out his hands, but the ball hit his thumb and bounced away.

Wincing from the pain of his jammed thumb, Chip breathed a sigh of relief. *I hope they don't run that play anymore,* he thought.

P.C. came over to congratulate him and, as usual, couldn't resist a tease. "Nice catch, Chip. You've got the hands of a surgeon."

"Oh, yeah?" snapped Rennie, getting slowly to his feet. "If you're so much better, how come you're not starting?"

"Come on, he's just kidding around," said Chip. "We always do."

Rennie said, "Whose side are you on, anyway? I wouldn't take that from a scrub."

"I'm not on anyone's side," Chip wanted to say. But he said nothing. He had the gnawing feeling he would have to make a choice soon. He felt a little hope as he saw P.C. shake his head at Rennie, more amused than angry. P.C. knew how it was, and he didn't let it bother him. If only Dan and Tom would keep playing it cool, too.

He looked over at Tom, who was scribbling something on the coach's clipboard. Ever since he had volunteered to be the manager, Tom had been exactly the problem Chip had expected. He couldn't tell a goalpost from a flagpole, and he wasn't afraid to ask the dumbest questions in his efforts to figure out the game. Compared to most boys on the field, Tom ran like a first grader. Worst of all, he still believed everything anybody told him. On Tom's first day at practice, Scot had told him that Coach Ray wanted all the tackling dummies in the front seat of his van. Tom had been struggling to get the second one in when Coach Ray had spotted him and run over to ask what he was doing. The whole team hooted for the next five minutes.

Chip always made a wide path around Tom at practice after that. *If Bruce and those guys don't like us being with subs, they'll really put up a stink about hanging around him,* he thought. Tom had bought his explanation that it was traditional on sports teams for the starters to spend most of practice time with other starters. But Chip knew that his new "buddies" were making fun of Tom. It had to hurt Tom that Chip was one of them.

For the next two weeks, Chip found himself looking over his shoulder whenever he talked to P.C. or Dan. He never called out to them, and he made sure he broke off all discussion between plays as soon as he saw the offense break the huddle. Meanwhile, the starters got worse. Some of them wouldn't speak to a player who wasn't in the Blue and White Club. Chip felt more trapped than ever. Although he loved being a starter, he welcomed the last day of practice before the final game against Madison.

As he sat on the outskirts of the Blue and White Club meeting, he started picking his name off his helmet. These meetings had become a pain. He worked off the last of the tape and started rubbing off the glue. Once he looked up and saw Bronc looking at them from a distance. Immediately, he went back to his helmet cleaning. *Why does he always make me feel guilty every time he looks at me?* Chip thought glumly. *I'm not even the one who's causing the trouble.*

The talk had turned to one of the club's favorite subjects, Eric. Actually, Chip hadn't had any problem with his old enemy for quite a while. Eric was learning a new position. It took all of his strength and stubborn determination to hold his own against the larger boys

112

in the line. Chip had tried to give the guy a break now and then. He even told him, "Nice tackle," once, but he couldn't tell if Eric had heard it.

As much as he still disliked Eric, Chip had to admit that most of the recent scraps between Eric and teammates were started by the good old Blue and White. They had singled him out spitefully by keeping him out of the club even though he was a starter. Since Forest Grove lost its last game to McKinley, Eric could no longer be blamed for spoiling their perfect record with his penalty. But the enemies he had made had not grown kinder.

"Hey, keep it down until the bald monkey gets to his truck," Bruce told everyone. The group fell silent as Bronc walked across the parking lot. When the truck roared off, Bruce said, "OK, everyone got the plan? Tomorrow's the day we give Eric all the publicity he deserves. 'Eric Youngquist is a dork!' Write that everywhere you can get away with it. Lockers, halls, books, sheets of paper, buses, bathrooms, the whole works."

"I don't know," said Roosevelt. "We could get in trouble for that."

"It's not like vandalism," said Bruce. "We're only using chalk. Just a one-day thing to put him in his place."

"Hey! I've got a great idea!" Scot said. "We could kick the whole thing off with a grand opening. You know, Eric lives down the hill from me with his grandparents. Well, they have a big yard, and I've seen Eric raking for a couple of weeks out there. He's almost done; he must have fifty bags out there. Why don't we go and rip 'em up, and spread 'em back on the lawn!"

To Chip's horror, the starters all liked the idea. Chip sank back on the sidewalk, watching Scot take sweeping bows to the laughter and applause.

"Pretty good, huh, Chip?" said Bruce, poking Chip

113

in the ribs.

Chip faked a nod. "But how am I supposed to explain this to my parents?"

"Good point!" shouted Bruce. "Hey, everybody! Just tell your folks that the team wants to go over a few last-minute details before the last game. Meet at ten minutes after dark at Scot's house."

10
The New Left Linebacker

"So how dark does it have to be before it's 'dark'?" muttered Chip as he pulled back the drapes of the living room window. The sun had set, but he could still make out the autumn colors blending into the shadows. Frowning, he looked at his own front yard littered ankle deep by the fallings of a large maple. He guessed it would take nearly ten minutes for him to run over to Scot's. If he was going to go, he'd have to start soon.

He walked back and forth across the carpet, trying to figure out how he had gotten himself into the mess. He still couldn't stand Eric. There was no getting around the fact that Eric had brought his troubles on himself. The guy deserved everything they were going to do to him and more. Besides, if there was one person on earth who had a right to revenge on Eric, it was Chip. He tried to bring up those memories of when Eric had been at his cruelest, and he at his most helpless.

But those moments kept fading out of focus. Instead, he kept seeing Dan and Bronc as they talked about Eric's problems. *As if he were the victim instead of the guy who started it all,* sniffed Chip, trying to dismiss the thoughts. It didn't work. The picture that kept coming back was that of Chip in Eric's place. If Eric really was like him, if he was as desperate for approval as Chip was, then it was all just brutal. He hated that smirk of Eric's. How would it be to have twelve or fifteen of those leering faces haunting you wherever you went? How could a guy even face going to school, knowing most of the class despised you and the rest knew enough to stay away from you?

What's the use? Chip thought. *Even if I don't show up tonight, there's still all the business with the signs tomorrow.* He went to the kitchen and prowled for a snack to take with him. Jill was the only one home. She looked up from the table, where she had spread out her schoolbooks.

"Must be a really big game tomorrow," she said. "I don't think I've ever seen you so nervous."

"No bigger than usual," Chip said. "We've already lost two games, so we can't win the title anyway." He hunted in the back closet for his jacket.

Jill shrugged as she ripped out a sheet of notebook paper. "Well, you could have fooled me. You're acting just like I feel before the most nerve-racking games of the year."

Sure, Miss Perfect gets nervous before games, Chip thought as he tried to unwedge the stuck zipper in his jacket. As soon as he thought it, though, he felt small. *Why pick on her? I got myself into this mess.* Just as he was about to step out the door, he saw her back as she flipped through the pages of a book. Suddenly, he felt he had to talk to someone. He felt torn in so many ways that he couldn't stand it anymore.

"When you're on a team, do the players get along?" he asked.

"I don't know. I guess so," she said, frowning at the interruption. "Everyone can't be close friends with everyone, but we usually have a good time together."

Chip felt so tired he slumped into a chair across from Jill. "Well, we've had problems. Boy, have we had problems!" He was sure Jill wouldn't know what he was talking about. She did the right things; her teams got along. But even when he finally started to gain some success, he was a failure. For the next five minutes he told her the history of the season, and he found himself talking faster and faster, as if he no longer could keep it under control.

Jill listened silently. When Chip finished with his story and the problem of the Blue and White Club, he was as stunned by what he saw as he was with the fact that he had just spilled it out. Jill looked worried, and swallowing wasn't coming easily.

"Wow!" she started, breathing heavily. "No wonder you acted that way all night! I wish I could give you an easy answer. I suppose you've thought about doing what *you* think is right without worrying about the others?"

"That's easy for you to say!" Chip retorted, resting his chin on his knuckles. "No matter what you do, everyone knows you're great. If I was like you, I could just snap my fingers and call the whole mess off."

Jill relaxed into a warm smile. "Boy, I didn't know you had me up on such a pedestal. You think it's easy for me to block out what other people think? Why do you think I came so close to quitting the team last week?"

Chip could hardly believe it. "You did?" As he

117

thought about it, though, nobody in the family had even brought up the subject of volleyball lately. "You? How come?"

"Same kind of thing you're talking about. In fact, you sounded so much like me when you first started telling me you were going crazy, I thought you found out about me and were making fun." She sighed. "Pressure. People were expecting more and more from me. There I was, running my tail off, trying to live up to their expectations, like you're trying to live up to what the starters think of you. Well, let me tell you: It doesn't matter how hard you try to please them, you won't win. I had that one bad game and we lost, and everyone wanted to know what was the matter with me. And then there's Dad! You should see him when I have an important match."

"Oh, I know about that," said Chip.

"He'd get so worked up that I got upset trying to do well just so he wouldn't get upset if we lost." She sat back. "It got so hard to please everyone that pretty soon I hated the whole thing. I told Dad and Mrs. Campbell that I thought I should quit."

Chip could hardly believe anyone else felt the same pressures he did, much less Jill. "So what happened? What did you do?"

"First, Dad and I talked it out. He was good about it, too. He apologized and said he loves us and is proud of us. That he just gets carried away sometimes, wishing the best for us."

"So did that take care of it?" asked Chip. He knew just talking with Dad wasn't going to solve his problem.

"Are you kidding?" said Jill. "The big problem was at school. Everyone was talking about what I could do, and how we were a cinch to win this and that. I was always worrying about blowing it, or what people would think if we didn't win. I just couldn't take being

118

pulled around. Well, they talked me out of quitting, but I still feel caught in the same trap."

She threw her pencil down hard as she leaned her chair against the wall. *So it's still bugging her,* Chip thought.

Jill went on. "I happened to mention it to the youth pastor at church, Pastor Wagner. He said I'm acting as though I'm not worth anything unless I do this or win that or please so-and-so. And it's so stupid; doing those things or acting that way doesn't make you different or more important. Pastor Wagner said that God accepts us the way we are, and if God accepts us, we don't have to prove anything to anyone. We're freed up to go out and play hard, have fun, help others, and do what really needs to be done. He said when you let yourself get pulled along by something you don't believe in, you're not your real self anymore."

Chip wrinkled his brow.

"I know what you're thinking," Jill said, laughing at his expression. "It's one thing to *say* you have to live up to your own standards, but it's easier to say it than to do it." She suddenly blushed. "Well, I've done it now. If I can *say* all that to a little brother, of all people, maybe I really *do* believe it!"

Chip knew he'd have to hurry if he wanted to get to Scot's on time. The fastest way was to run through the trail behind the swamp and up over the tracks to the hill. Although it was dark, there were enough lights from the houses surrounding the small swamp that he had no problem sticking to the trail.

It was better that he took that way and didn't use the streets, because he was so lost in thought he wasn't paying attention to anything around him. Once he had broken the ice with Jill, it had been easy enough to talk. But she was right. To do something about the problem was another story.

I haven't done anything I really wanted since I stepped in that locker room door back at the start, he thought. *Haven't even said anything I believed, either, except sometimes with Dan and P.C. Sure, Eric and Bruce and those guys started this whole mess. But I'm the one who let myself get caught in it. And it's all because I get scared. So scared that I throw away everything I really believe about God and what's right. Eric's the only one with any guts; he stands up to the whole lot of them.*

Without remembering anything about being on the swamp trail, he found himself crossing the tracks. He must have scrambled pretty hard up the hill, because he had a side ache. Automatically checking both ways for trains, he cut a shortcut onto a street.

It'd sure be easier if Eric wasn't such a creep, he thought. Then it hit him, so hard that he stopped in the middle of the street. *Who are you kidding, Demory?* he thought. *Dan and Tom and P.C. aren't creeps, and I've been treating them the same way.*

For the moment, Jill had pumped him up enough to challenge the Blue and White. He wasn't at all sure that would last, though, once he ran into Bruce and the others. In fact, he didn't have any idea of what he was going to do then. He crossed a street and went half a block further. He felt hot, but the drops of sweat on his face cooled quickly in the night breeze. Then he saw them. Everyone was there in Scot's yard. "God, help!" he whispered, and crossed the street to join them.

Eric's house was tucked into one of the few corners in the city. Although it was only minutes from downtown, a ridge on one side and the swamp on another had forced the road to twist into a dead end. There were three houses on the street, older ones by the looks of the porches and peeling paint. Eric's was the first in line.

Chip hadn't believed Scot's report of fifty bags of leaves. But he saw quickly that it was no exaggeration. It was a double lot, and there must have been twenty good-sized trees growing on it. The house was set near to the curb, with most of the yard behind it. The backyard was entirely fenced, except at the rear, where it spilled off down a hill into the swamp.

"This is the place," grinned Scot. Unlike most of the city's blocks, this one was mostly out of the range of streetlights; any light that would have hit the houses was smothered by all the trees.

"The bags must be near the garage, don't you think?" said Bruce, crouching low by the fence and signaling the others to do the same. "We'll have to be quiet about it. Why don't we circle behind the garage, get the bags, and dump them way in that dark corner by the back?"

"Yeah, less chance of getting caught," said Rennie. Scot led the way, followed by Bruce and then a string of others who looked around hesitatingly before following. Chip had meant to say something by now. But as the crouching group trickled toward the garage, he knew he just couldn't. He couldn't risk being ridiculed and snubbed just for Eric's sake. Not by himself. He wasn't a superhero; he just couldn't face them all alone. Near tears as he waited for the last person to go before him, he noticed that the other person was actually waiting for him. Roosevelt still sat on his haunches, eyes darting from the house to the group circling toward the garage.

Chip remembered the tackle's simple shake of the head during the practice when Bruce had whispered to Roosevelt about Dan. He realized, as he watched Roosevelt signal him forward, that he had been holding his breath for a long while. Letting the air out, he decided that this would be his chance. He felt as though he were plunging into an icy stream when he opened his mouth and said, "Wait a minute."

It wasn't long before the Blue and White Club

121

returned to the darkest corner of the yard. The long line of figures scurrying along with big loads on their backs reminded Chip of ants carting home food from a cupboard. Roosevelt had found what he was looking for, and returned from the other side of the house just before the others arrived.

Chip's heart was pounding as he took one of the rakes from Roosevelt. Although he dreaded each approaching step of his teammates, he refused to look up from his work. Even when he heard whisperings from the darkness behind him, he kept sweeping the leaves. Finally, they must have recognized him, or more likely recognized Roosevelt, since it was hard to mistake his large form even in this light.

"Have you guys lost your minds?" said Scot in a whisper.

"Probably," croaked Chip, sweeping his small pile toward Roosevelt's larger one.

"We figured this was getting out of hand," said Roosevelt.

"You picked a fine time to say that!" said Bruce, slamming his two bags to the ground. "I didn't hear anyone crying about it this afternoon."

"Better late than never," said Chip, finally looking up. It was eerie seeing all those shadows and no faces. There was no way of telling what everyone was thinking of all this.

"So maybe you don't like the idea," came a whisper that sounded like it might be Rennie. "Why come down and rake his yard?"

Chip hoped Roosevelt would answer, but the tackle silently kept on raking.

"We didn't *plan* it. Just seemed like a good idea at the moment. Look, we thought the idea of this club was fun at first," Chip said. "But look what's going on! Half the team hates the other half. About all we've done is come up with new ways to dump on everyone

122

else."

"Come on," scoffed Bruce. "You hated Eric before the club started."

Chip's knees were shaking. As far as he could tell, he wasn't getting anywhere. Stubbornly, he went back to raking. "Maybe. That doesn't mean I have to act as mean and stupid as he did."

Chip felt a little better as Roosevelt finally spoke. "I never liked gangin' up on guys. Chip and I got talkin' about it at the last few minutes. This Blue and White stuff is gettin' too stuck up." He tied off the two bags he had finished stuffing and said, "We figured the club should do something to make up for the damage it's done before we break it up. It looks like there's about twenty bags worth of leaves left in the yard. Here's my contribution." He threw the bags at Scot's feet, hoisted himself over the fence, and walked off.

Chip felt like rushing after him. With Roosevelt gone, he didn't know what would happen. But he hadn't finished his second bag of leaves, so he kept at it. Something rushed past his ear, making him jump back. Chip saw that it was a bag of leaves, and the boy who had thrown it was coming toward him.

"Here's *my* contribution," Bruce sneered, ripping open the bag with a hard kick. After booting the bag around the yard, spreading leaves everywhere, he took his other bag and did the same. Brushing past Chip without looking at him, he, too, hopped the fence and left.

Chip shrank back toward the corner of the yard as three others followed Bruce, and then another ran after them. *Well, you've done it now, Demory*, he thought. *You just joined Eric on their hit list.* But, with his eyes growing more used to the darkness, he could make out that at least the four followers hadn't ripped open their bags. And none of the rest had moved. All were standing with their bags resting on the ground beside them,

123

making them appear as though they were waiting at a bus stop with their suitcases.

Chip almost jumped when he heard the first whisper. It was Scot, of all people. "You've got a point, kid," he said, picking up Roosevelt's dropped rake. "If yours is a stupid idea, at least it's no stupider than anything else we've done." As if on cue, the others gathered around, helping stuff bags while they waited for a turn at a rake. Chip stared dumbly at them, and even more so at Rennie, who took his bag from him and finished twisting the top.

When Scot finished his two bags, he stepped toward Chip and pulled him out of earshot of the others. "Has Bronc been talking to you?"

"Not for a while," Chip answered.

Scot shrugged. "Just wondering. He's been after me a bit lately. He says part of being a good quarterback is being a team leader. He never really says what he's getting at, but somehow . . ."

He left the sentence hanging, but Chip nodded in agreement. *So it's not just me,* he thought. *Bronc's been working on everyone.*

They were back under the lights at the municipal park for the last game against Madison. There wasn't much grass left in the middle of the field. But somehow the bright lights and sharply marked hash marks made the field appear inviting.

Chip waited until Bronc was through giving instructions to Tom, and then approached him. "Say, coach?"

"Yeah, player?" grinned Bronc.

"I've got a suggestion for a lineup change."

"Everyone wants to be a coach. Well, you can give it to me if you can do it in forty-five seconds or less," said Bronc, checking his watch. "Just promise you won't feel bad if I tell you no."

124

Chip swallowed hard as he looked at the shimmering blue jerseys of the Madison team warming up. "I think you should give Dan a try at my linebacker job."

Bronc's eyebrows shot up. "That's very noble of you, but you've earned the spot."

As Bronc turned away, Chip grabbed him by the shoulder. Although it took him a bit longer than his forty-five second time limit, he told Bronc all about Dan's keen instincts and clever deductions. Bronc mulled it over awhile. "Dan figured all that out? Well, ordinarily I'd say he's too slow to be a linebacker and of course he's too thin to be a good lineman. But a guy can make up for some of that with smarts and desire. You know, he never looked too coordinated. But then nobody looks too sharp when they're up against Roosevelt." He paused for a second. "I'll let you know. Meanwhile, for heaven's sake, tell Roosevelt and Scot that they're tipping off the plays. Most likely there's no one on Madison as smart as Dan, but you never know."

Coach Ray gathered the team a few minutes later to make his usual pregame speech. He cleared his throat and looked down at his notebook. "We've got just one lineup change I want to announce. Atkinson and Demorg will alternate at left linebacker. Atkinson, take the first series."

Dan looked at Chip in disbelief and pointed a questioning finger at his chest. Chip nodded and winked. *Quit feeling so proud of yourself, Demory,* he scolded himself. *You should have given him some credit a long time ago.* But it didn't stop him from grinning.

Dan had a few problems at first. He wasn't as fast as most linebackers, and a couple of times Madison runners beat him to the outside for good gains. As the game went on, he lined up further to the outside and was able to stop those plays.

Midway through the third quarter, Forest Grove led 20-14. Standing on the sidelines between P.C. and

Tom, Chip nervously watched as the unbeaten Madison team drew close to another score. With two powerful runners and a quarterback who could throw well, they had been averaging over four touchdowns a game.

"When do you go in again?" Tom asked.

"Next defensive series." Seeing Tom's blank look, he added, "The next time our offense turns the ball over to the other team."

"How come that player is waving his hand?" Tom asked.

"That's Dan," said P.C. "Who knows what he's up to. Maybe he's trying to shoo away the only fly stupid enough to still be outdoors this time of year."

Chip held back a giggle as he saw Tom nod solemnly. It had been funny watching those two all game. Tom seemed to have a bottomless well of questions, and P.C. an equally full supply of smart answers. In all this time, P.C. hadn't noticed that Tom was taking his jokes seriously.

"Don't believe a thing that character says," he told Tom. "I think Dan's probably figured out something in the offensive setup, and he's signaling the rest."

The three watched as Madison tried a pass play into the end zone. The quarterback aimed a soft pass toward his right end, who was cutting across the middle. Chip was already slumping in defeat as he saw that the receiver was clearly beyond Rennie.

But the pass never got there. A tall frame stretched high in the air to make a fingertip grab.

"Interception!" yelled P.C. and Chip at the same time. The whole team jumped around whooping, while Dan ran off the field cradling his prize.

"Hey, I think they're going to need that thing back on the field," said Bronc, snatching the football away from the excited linebacker and firing it back to an official. "Tremendous play, Dan," he added. "Tremendous."

126

Dave Atkinson, dressed in street clothes, hopped over on his crutches to join the group. "How did you figure that out?" he asked his brother. "That wasn't your man. What were you doing back there?"

"I know it wasn't my man," grinned Dan. "But I found out that whenever the ball was going to go to that end, he'd always adjust his mouthpiece after taking his stance. You know, really wedge it in there tight. When I saw him do it, it seemed like a good chance to take."

Bronc stared at them, one of the rare times Chip had seen him stop in midchew. Then he turned to Chip and said, "I think Rennie could use a breather. Take over for a few plays."

"No problem," said Chip, strapping on his helmet. It wasn't until he reached the huddle that he realized the Forest Grove team was on offense! That meant that Chip was at running back! A wave of fear swept over him as Scot called out the play. But by the time he lined up, he had remembered the system. After blocking for Bruce, who hadn't spoken all night, on two plays, he leaned into the huddle to listen to the next play selection.

"Forty-two Red on four," said Scot.

Quit grinning, you idiot, he said to himself as he lined up. *Everyone in the whole park will know you're carrying this play.* He charged forward at the snap, saw a slim opening in the line and ran into it. Two linebackers closed quickly and wrapped him tightly in their arms, but he wriggled and squirmed for an extra yard. By the time he picked himself up, Rennie was waiting for him.

"Nice run," he said, slapping him on the shoulder pads.

Chip nodded and jogged to the sidelines. Seeing his dad standing alone near the 20-yard line, he veered over to him so suddenly that he bumped into a dirt-covered uniform near the end of the squad. It was Eric's.

"Sorry," Chip said. "Didn't have my turn signal on."

"Nice run," mumbled Eric, so softly Chip could barely hear it.

"Way to play tough," Chip answered. Then he jogged over to his dad, who was battling the effects of a cold with a pocketful of tissues. "That was fun!" said Chip.

"Enjoyed it myself," sniffled his dad. "You got one more yard than you should have gotten." As they watched the Forest Grove offense drive slowly down-field for another score, Dad said, "Looks like you got the game won."

"No problem," shrugged Chip. "We had it won before the game even started." As his dad's laugh was cut short by a brief coughing fit, Chip added, to himself, *In more ways than one.*